PLAGUE

of the

LOST
ONES

PLAGUE

of the

LOST
ONES

L. J. Black

This book is dedicated to all those affected by the
COVID-19 pandemic, past, present, and future.

For Jaxsie

Plague
of the
Lost Ones

1

CREATOR OF THE PLAGUE

One drop.

A scientist in his early fifties stands at a lab hood in a full hazmat suit reminiscent of those seen in the movie *Contagion*. It's no wonder given he is working with one of the most dangerous viral agents ever developed. The lab is cold and even inside his suit he can feel it. He works slowly, moving single drops of solution from its storage case to smaller vials for transport. Soon this lab would be the only place on Earth that held the key to this plague.

Pipettes can be finicky, so he takes his time. One spill could be lethal if it gets on his suit even. He had tested himself years ago and knew he carried the genetic marker the disease targeted in humans. While it wouldn't necessarily kill a human, he did not want to be part of a clinical trial to test that out.

He finishes the transfer and gingerly disposes of the pipette tip before setting the instrument down. Only after he has closed all five vials does he finally let out a tight breath of relief.

"All done Roland?" a voice asks in his earpiece.

He looks to his left, out through the large window where a small group has gathered. At the forefront is his colleague and the source of the voice, a woman with red hair and a furrowed brow. She sequenced the genome needed to create this virus, as well as developed an antiviral treatment and vaccine if anyone in the lab were exposed. Given that Roland carries the gene, he is grateful for her expertise in that matter.

"Finished," Roland answers. He carefully slides the vials into a plastic carrying case exactly fitting their size. Once secured, he places the case in the double-sealed chamber and closes the door on his side. One press of a button and the chamber evacuates its air. On the other side one of his colleagues pushes another button to restore air and gently opens the chamber to remove the vials.

Roland makes his way to the airlock at the back of the room and steps through. Decontamination runs, blowing his suit with aerosol disinfectant. A red light in front of him switches off and a green one turns on. He approaches the door and steps outside. He unhooks his airline from his back and begins to remove his suit.

Almost compulsively, Roland runs his hand through salt-and-pepper hair. He is too young to be graying, but with the things he's seen and what he knows at forty-one he is slowly going completely silver. The bit of hair that hasn't grayed out is a dark once-brown color, a near-identical match for his eyes. He changes from his lab clothes, a simple t-shirt and thin shorts. The suits get hot when wearing them for any period of time. The back of his shirt was wet with sweat.

About twenty minutes later, he joins his colleagues and the group who had been watching in a laboratory meeting room. He glances around the cold room with the glass walls overlooking the lab and takes a seat at the metal table, the chair rolling easily on the smooth floor. Everything about this room is as sterile as the lab.

"Roland, I was just expressing my gratitude for the hard work you and Kathryn have been putting in," a man to the left of the head of the table says. He gestures to the red-headed woman who had been watching him earlier. "I was suggesting since we know you and several of the lab technicians carry the gene, that you all be vaccinated so there are no accidents to worry about."

A small amount of relief seeps from Roland. He had been

worried about not just himself but the others working on the project becoming exposed to the virus and jeopardizing the hard work they had put in. "I feel that would be prudent," he says with little show of his actual relief. "I doubt a lab accident would keep us as under-the-radar as we need to be."

Kathryn's brown eyes meet his for a brief moment. They had had that conversation just a few days ago, that the entire reason for being here could implode if they do not take more precautions. The woman at the head of the table, their fearless and also ruthless leader, nods in agreement. She tucks a strand of brown hair behind her ear, the scar on her hand made more apparent in that moment. Her features are plain as are her clothes. Her suit is passably corporate enough with the kind of tidiness that ensures she goes unnoticed. That is their job here—to go unnoticed.

When she speaks it is softly but with conviction. "We should inoculate our whole lab group, regardless of if they have the gene. It will help prevent any variants from attacking baseline humans." She looks at the man to her left who had spoken before. "Do you have any objections?"

"None at all," he says with a dismissive wave. "Our people should be protected and rewarded for their hard work."

She turns to the three others seated together across from Roland and Kathryn. The two men are wiry thinktank-type nerds with slim state-of-the-art laptops in front of them. The woman flashes green eyes across the table at Roland but otherwise chooses to avoid eye-contact. Her face is quite forgettable, as are the rest of them around the table. While they were chosen for their brains, the company encourages them to avoid any obvious features or remarkable fashion statements to keep from standing out. Similarly they try not to completely memorize their features or associate with each other outside of the lab. No need to create connections.

Their leader asks the three, "Are we ready to deploy?"

The three exchange furtive glances, the woman lifting the tablet in front of her. The thin pane of reinforced glass looks transparent, but the technology prevents anyone but the genetically keyed user from seeing what is on the panel. Roland knew she left the panel in her office every night. As far as the public knows, the technology doesn't exist yet.

"All forces in place," she says without saying where. No one but the strike team knows the locations where the virus is to be deployed. The two men next to her nod curtly but say nothing. Roland can't remember if he has ever heard their voices.

"Then if we are all in agreement, we will proceed," their leader says. She looks at Kathryn and adds, "Vaccinate the entire lab staff before they leave for the day." To the strike team she says, "Order deployment."

Roland clears his throat and says, "One of our staff is out

today, but we can get him vaccinated in the morning."

Their leader nods, acknowledging. "If that's all, I think we'll leave it there. As usual, you know the penalties for indiscretion. Proceed carefully."

With that they all stand and leave the table, exiting the meeting room one at a time. Roland follows Kathryn back to the lab. She pulls a collection of vials out of a locked cabinet and calls the lab team over. She explains the vaccination procedure and begins to draw up doses for everyone. Without argument, knowing the dangerous nature of their work, each lab member rolls up a sleeve and waits to be vaccinated.

With that the last piece is set in motion. Roland leaves the lab at the end of the day with a feeling of completion to his work. In reality their work has only just begun.

2

AROUND THE CORNER

Adin resists the urge to stand up and stretch, tired as he is of crouching behind the dumpster in the alley. The smell doesn't bother him that much, but sitting still for hours does. The sun has fully set now and the alley is mostly shrouded in darkness. The light from the streetlamp at the end of the alley doesn't quite reach this far down.

A lone figure comes up from the crossing alley and walks around the corner, also sticking to the shadows. One sniff of the air and Adin knows the newcomer. He waits till Lairlux comes closer then stands up. If Lairlux were human, she would have been startled. But her unique eyes can penetrate the dark better than Adin's werewolf eyes can.

"Adin," she says softly. The creature's eyes flicker red briefly before going back to their ordinary brown. Most humans would not sense the power or strength in her. She works to conceal it in any case.

"Have the rest arrived?" she asks.

"Not since I got here," Adin replies.

"Then let me conceal us so you no longer have to crouch," Lairlux says. Adin stretches his legs gratefully as a shimmer in the air surrounds them. Lairlux barely made a gesture to conjure the concealment shield, her proficiency due to her parentage of both witch and demon. Adin is not aware of another witch-demon hybrid, but it does not surprise him. The species rarely commingle, much less mate.

"How have you been? How is the pack?" Lairlux asks.

Their relationship has always been a friendly one and Adin has felt no uneasiness around her. "I have been well, and the pack is managing," he says, referring to the Nightstar pack. "The rumors have everyone on edge, but I supposed that's why we are having this meeting tonight."

Adin is no high ranking member of his pack, but his friendliness with Lairlux and those of other species make him something of an ambassador. So Alpha Radcliff sent him to this clandestine meeting of the species. Part of him felt he was joining the ranks of the espionage elite, a feeling exacerbated by the shield and the dark of night around them.

A creature making their way down the alley draws both of their attention. Across from them in the adjoining alley Lairlux came down, a door inset into the wall and shut with a heavy bar across the back is the focus of the newcomer. The newcomer turns their head in the direction of the pair and squints at them as if they could see them behind the shield. A flash of a car's headlight on her black hair and both Adin and Lairlux relax a tad recognizing the newcomer. It is likely she did see right through Lairlux's shield.

With a nod to Adin, Lairlux drops the shield and they cautiously step out of the shadows. None of them say anything but together they approach the door. The newcomer raises a fist and knocks. The sounds of movement inside are followed by a metallic scraping sound. A tiny porthole Adin could swear wasn't there a moment ago opens. The face meeting them is unremarkable but the unsettled feeling Adin gets in his stomach means the person is undeniably full demon.

Without a word the demon shuts the porthole—the outlines of which immediately disappear—and the door swings outward slowly. The newcomer leads them in followed by Lairlux with Adin bringing up the rear. Once past the threshold all three know better than to take more than a few steps inside as the door shuts behind them. The low red lights reveal the vestibule and the marks on the floor on which they stand. A voice from the edge of the room says, "Identify yourself and your species for the wards."

"Kai Soriano. Witch," the newcomer starts.

"Lairlux Roseburg. Demon-witch hybrid."

"Adin Kennel. Werewolf."

The marks on the floor light up beneath them and glow a menacing red then blue then a softer whitish green. They seem to have passed the test.

"Good to see you Lairlux," the voice says. The demon who greeted them at the door steps forward and gives a chilling smile Adin thinks is meant to be friendly.

"Orguth," Lairlux says with a half smile. She embraces the demon and says, "How's the horde doing?"

Orguth chuckles. "About the same. Come by for dinner sometime. The offspring would like to see you."

Lairlux smiles warmly and nods in agreement promising she would. The small talk is cut off as Kai leads them through a set of heavy curtains and the door at the end of the vestibule. Beyond the door is what could only be described as a seedy bar. The space is hidden from human eyes and only some creatures know about it at all. The bar hosts all species on the stipulation that any disputes be kept outside.

Along the far wall, a heavy wooden bar flanked by padded stools stands empty except for the proprietor behind it washing glasses. Behind him a mirror lines the wall behind the bar, the name of the bar etched into its glass. The reflection of the odd group looks back at them and Adin smiles, his reflection interrupted by the words ALCHEMIST BREWING CO. He admits to himself the three of them would look very out of place on a street during daylight.

The proprietor smiles at them and waves them in. The small group weaves through a half dozen tables and heads to the right of the bar where the proprietor meets them at a carved Dutch door. Without anything more than a nod, he opens the door for them and they go through. This is not their first meeting here.

Adin pulls the door shut behind him and they enter the small room that would normally host private parties in the creature community. They have made this their meeting place by default. It's not considered unusual for any of them to be seen entering or leaving the establishment.

A glance around the room takes in the half dozen others gathered there. They usually keep these meetings small and inconspicuous. It's an unspoken rule that they will come together en masse if there ever were a real emergency. The fact that twice the number of creatures than normal are waiting for them suggests the seriousness of the current situation.

Adin, Lairlux, and Kai all take seats around the table. Across the table are another witch, three werewolves from other packs, another demon, and one person who could only be a spirit of some kind. Adin recognizes some of them, but the spirit and the demon in particular are unknown to him.

The group nods at each other. Adin gives a brief smile to the werewolf he recognizes, a she-wolf named Chloe Plank who comes from a pack in the neighboring state. She gives a small smile back, but there is a grimness in her eyes that betrays the seriousness of the situation.

Asa Shertz, the witch who called the meeting, wastes no time getting down to business. She starts by saying, "We've been getting reports of an alarming nature in the past few weeks. I asked Sorkelen—" she gestures at the demon— "and Oriphine—" she gestures at the spirit— "to be here so we can spread the word as far as possible."

She clears her throat and brings out a short sheaf of papers. "We've been getting reports of an illness that seems to only be targeting creatures. It was first noticed in the witches of New York City and in a small cluster outside of San Francisco. We've since confirmed there is a cluster in Europe and one in Asia as well," she says reading from notes in front of her.

Kai picks up from where Asa leaves off. Her presence suddenly makes sense to Adin. Not only is she a healing witch, but she is also a doctor in the human world. She works in a hospital in Atlanta and has connections in the CDC. "When we first identified the disease we thought it was confined to witches only, but we have seen some humans getting mild forms of the disease. Especially non-magical human relatives of witches. And then about two weeks ago we identified a case in the werewolf pack in New York City as well as in the pack in the Adirondacks."

Adin's eyes go to the two male werewolves across from him. Both of them look back at him and the expressions on their faces are enough to tell him they had not heard this news.

"Since then we have identified cases in several native people's packs and in the Loner Werewolf Registry and the Solitary Witch Network as well," Kai continues. Knots form in Adin's stomach, the grim reality of something spreading this quickly before them.

"Thus far, we have about 30 cases in the witch population, 23 in the werewolf population, and half a dozen mild cases among humans," Asa says. "We don't think it actively targets humans. We managed to get samples of the humans' DNA. As I'm sure you all are aware, with the exception of spirits we all have genetic markers that make us creatures. These humans have a small amount of those markers, whether werewolf, witch, or demon. Not enough for them or any of their most recent four or five generations to be a creature, but enough to carry one or two minor traits."

Sorkelen raises his hand as if to ask a question. Asa nods and he asks, "What about vampires? Have we heard anything from them? And have you noticed any cases in demons?"

Asa glances at Kai who takes out her notebook and pages through to a handwritten list. Adin, sitting next to her, can see the last name and first initial of every positive case and a note next to them of their species. "I have one case that is possibly a demon," she says. "And I've been in touch with the vampire community, but as you know they are fairly reclusive. I got a message from the Royal Court of North America and they will get back to me tomorrow or the next day." She glances at Asa who looks surprised. "The Royal Court may send an envoy down to work with us or have us come up there."

A tense silence meets her words. The vampires' concern over the situation only increases the seriousness in the room. Why would seemingly immortal creatures worry? Adin glances at Oriphine and notices the spirit's knitted brows.

Kai glances back at her notes. "My contacts at the CDC have been made aware of the situation and are actively tracking the illnesses, including the creature numbers in the human numbers to make the tracking more legitimate. The creatures working at the CDC and in medical facilities around the country have been alerted to the illness."

"Why have we not been made aware of this before?" one of the male werewolves asks.

"It is new," Kai answers. "The first case was about three weeks ago, but it wasn't identified as a creature disease until early last week. This is our fourth meeting like this."

Adin's eyebrows go up and he exchanges another look with Lairlux. Her brown eyes flash red for a moment, but there is worry there. Understandably she looks upset.

"What would you like us to do?" Sorkelen asks, his expression betraying his concern.

"Reach out to your contacts and spread the word," Asa answers. "We have reached out to other sects of demons, but you are the first night demon, for example. The more species and creatures aware, the more we can get ahead of this."

"Are there any treatments?" the other werewolf asks.

Kai lets out a tight breath. "Not at the moment." She glances at Chloe. "And we suspect the more genetic markers, the more devastating the disease. Chloe?"

Chloe straightens up to speak to the group. "As you know our Luna is the daughter of another pack's Alpha. She carries strong Alpha blood in her line, going back a hundred years or more," Adin nods, knowing this but also knowing the explanation is for the others in the group. "Well the Alpha and Luna's daughter is gravely ill." She swallows looking down at notes on her phone. "The results of Esyn Margrave's genetic sequencing showed an unusually but not unexpectedly high amount of genetic markers for the Alpha lines. She was expected to be the first female Alpha of Swifttooth pack."

The use of past tense brings a chilling silence to the room.

"Is there no hope of her recovering?" Adin asks, appalled at the idea. Esyn is only about seven years old, but precocious for her age. So many in the werewolf community know of her.

Kai's expression is as grim as Chloe's. "There is always hope, but she is the worst case we have seen by far." She pauses and glances at Chloe before saying, "She only contracted the disease four days ago and we are already considering putting her on a ventilator."

Adin swallows, his throat suddenly dry.

"Are any of the others on ventilators?"

"Several," Asa says. "We are not sure if anyone has died from the disease yet as we are still tracking down the rural creatures. But for several of them, the outlook is not good." She pauses and looks at Kai.

"My contacts at the CDC are suggesting using preventative measures, such as wearing face masks and quarantining any infected to help reduce the infection rate," she says. "I realize this is asking a lot, especially since our various species' communities are close knit." A general murmur of agreement runs through the group and Adin glances at Chloe who nods gravely. It would be difficult, but given the seriousness of the disease, extremely necessary.

"The Alpha and his family, as well as any person in close contact with them the past few weeks, are quarantining now," Chloe confirms. "Our pack has emergency protocols in place for situations like this."

The other werewolves sitting next to her exchange dark looks, but don't object.

"What can my people do for you?" Oriphine asks suddenly. Even though Adin is looking directly at her, he is not sure he would be able to describe her later. Her skin is so glassy that it is almost translucent and her features while humanesque are not human at all. No spirit can pass for human without using serious magic to disguise themselves.

Asa glances at Kai before answering. "We are hoping you will take a look at some of the infected and get some of your fellow earth nymphs to do the same."

Oriphine nods, immediately understanding. "You believe it is partially supernatural in nature and not just a viral agent."

"In a sense," Kai answers. "It is definitely a viral agent. We are hoping to fully isolate and sequence it by next week. It is more a question of whether this is a vessel or tool to carry a supernatural attack."

The spirit's eyes go vague as she seems to contemplate the matter. "It wouldn't be completely unheard of to do such a thing," she says. "I am out-of-practice healer by any standard, but I know at least one individual who may be able to help. I will contact them to ask." She looks at Chloe and says, "In the meantime I feel it might be prudent to examine the Alpha's daughter."

Chloe nods. "I believe her parents would agree to that."

Kai nods. "We'll accompany you," she says, indicating herself and Asa. "And we should go soon, tomorrow if possible."

Chloe picks up her phone and shoots out a text, presumably to her Alpha. Like Adin, Chloe has taken up a position similar to that of an ambassador or diplomat. It seems she too was sent here on her Alpha's behalf. A moment later her phone lights up. "He says to come first thing in the morning, as soon as you can," she says after briefly reading the message.

Kai nods and glances at Asa. "We'll be there."

A brief silence falls over the group. "Are there any more questions or concerns?" Asa asks.

A few murmurs but generally everyone shakes a head or says no.

"Alright, we'll reconvene as necessary. Please be careful out there."

3

DINER AT NIGHT

The group rises from the table as they make their way through the door to the establishment. The proprietor exchanges a dark look with Adin as they pass. A few of them stay and get drinks at the bar, but Adin follows Lairlux out through the entrance. Kai, Asa, and Chloe have stayed behind with Oriphine, no doubt so they could be given instructions on how to get to Chloe's pack house. Locations of pack houses are not always common knowledge. Some packs, like Chloe's, prefer to keep their location to pack knowledge only.

Lairlux gives a warm farewell to Orguth on their way

through the vestibule. The demon gives Adin a mildly friendly nod and smile—a smile that sends a chill down his spine. For a death demon Orguth is remarkably friendly. Then again his restraint in his use of his abilities is likely why he got the job as doorman at Alchemist. Security isn't useful if you kill all your clientele.

Adin follows Lairlux out into the street, the door shutting behind them once they are through. For a moment the two of them just pause, standing in the dark alleyway. The moonless sky laden with rain clouds, it begins to drizzle as they stand there.

"Let's get a coffee at the usual place," Lairlux says suddenly, her voice soft. "I think we should talk."

Adin looks at her, sees her slightly haunted expression, and nods. She is his friend, and though she occasionally gives him the creeps, he always feels a sense of loyalty to her. Once, a long time ago, she saved him and he has never forgotten that. The act has been repaid multiple times over, but they stopped counting years ago. Now they help each other out of friendship.

As they turn the corner onto the street, a group of younger werewolves enter the alley, smiling and nodding at the strange pair. Adin does not recognize any of them, but he recognizes the youthful ignorance of the coming darkness. For a moment, he envies that.

He tugs the collar of his jacket up, the rain starting to fall earnestly now. Lairlux looks annoyed at the rain, but otherwise is not bothered by it. She does no more than tuck her hands into her coat's pockets and pull it tighter about herself. A few blocks down they come to the diner they usually frequent. A neon sign in the window advertises the coffee Adin suddenly feels he needs. He holds the door for Lairlux and the two step gratefully into the dry interior.

At the hostess's urging, they take a seat at a booth along the front windows but away from the doors. Another sign advertises pancakes in their window. As Lairlux shrugs out of her coat and hangs it on the convenient hook next to their booth, a human waitress, likely around twenty, comes to their table with menus and silverware. She smiles reflexively as they take the menus from her, the expression faltering slightly when Lairlux smiles back. The demon hybrid does a good job hiding her nature, but in close quarters it isn't always easy.

"Can I get you a drink?" the waitress asks.

"Some coffee please," Lairlux says.

"Me too, please," Adin agrees.

The waitress leaves and they look over the menus.

"Are you hungry?" Adin asks suddenly. He can always eat, but he feels it is rude to do so when his companion is not going to join him.

"Actually, I'm starving," she says. "I haven't eaten since I had lunch with my father and that was quite a while ago."

Adin nods, surprised by both the answer and the details she added. "We should go ahead and get some food. I don't have anywhere to be right now."

She smiles at him, and for once the genuineness completely overrides the demonic nature. "I think I'll order some pancakes," she says. "I miss my mom's cooking since I've stopped living at home."

Right then the waitress comes over with their coffee, placing two cups on the table and pouring till they are mostly full. She sets a bowl with individual creamers on the table as well before getting out a pad from her apron.

"Are you ready to order?" Her manner seems more open now, the moment of upset clearly forgotten or forgiven.

Adin gestures for Lairlux to go first. Her smile at the waitress is so genuine that the waitress smiles back with none of the apprehension of before. "Can you make banana pancakes?"

"Of course!" the waitress answers. "Would you like a short stack?"

"Yes, please. And two eggs, over medium, with bacon and hashbrowns on the side."

The waitress dutifully writes that down before turning to Adin.

"I'll take a stack of pancakes as well, but I'd like steak and eggs with mine," he says, glancing back at the menu. "Medium rare on the steak."

"How would you like the eggs?"

"Over medium."

"Hashbrowns ok with that?"

"Yes please, and a side of fruit so I don't feel like such a glutton."

That earned him a laugh and a head shake from Lairlux. She knows he has no shame with regard to his appetite.

"Alright, I'll get started on that right away," the waitress says. "Let me know if you need anything." She beams at both of them, takes their menus, and heads behind the counter.

Lairlux adds a creamer and a sugar to her coffee, something Adin does not do. They sip their drinks for a few minutes in silence. Outside the window an occasional person hurries by with an umbrella or a coat pulled tight. But mostly the street is deserted as the rain starts pouring down. The glowing lights of the street signs reflect on the growing puddles. The grayness of the atmosphere fits his mood.

The sound of Lairlux setting her coffee cup down brings him back to the moment.

"Are you worried?" she asks softly.

He meets her brown eyes, seeing no trace of the demon within for the moment. "I don't think it's sunk in enough yet to cause me worry. Are you?"

She pauses before answering. "I am getting there. Knowing the situation with Esyn makes me wonder how directly targeted I could be," she says.

The thought had crossed Adin's mind as well. Her father is the demon and her mother the witch, but that is only part of her reality. Her parents were a love match, a true partnership and cooperation that produced a loving if strange home for her upbringing. They are still together and up till six months ago Lairlux was living at home. She felt comfortable and welcome enough to stay there all through her college years. She only moved out to be closer to the coven grounds and the local demon horde she works with.

Adin reaches for her hand reflexively but pulls it back. Rather than shy away like she might have done so many times in the past, Lairlux reaches out and takes it. They had only touched a few times in the past and Adin is struck by how brief and passing those moments were. Once helping her up, another time so they wouldn't get separated in a crowd. Never with purpose and focus like now.

Her scent becomes more pronounced and around them the world falls away. His nose fills with the smell of the forest after rain and the pepperiness of nasturtium. He blinks as her hidden demonic traits surface for a moment, the red color blending with the brown eyes. A thin scar runs the length of her face crossing her right eye and ending down at her jaw. He had never seen it before.

All around me I see the layer under reality, she says in his mind. *I feel the power in me, the tug-of-war between light and dark. I feel my mother's strength and my father's will.*

Adin's eyes move away from her and he sees the diner as she sees it for a moment. The tiny touch of witch-power in their waitress, the man at the counter with a dark shadow over him, and even the power in the rain outside. It is a marvel she distinguishes the tangible from the unseen at all.

He looks down at his own hand, the thin sheen of the purple glow wrapped around him. He wonders if all werewolves have a purplish glow.

How can I ever feel safe again when I have this in me? she asks.

Adin meets her eyes, the fear there scaring him more than anything.

She lets go of his hand, returning everything to normal. Only a few seconds have passed. The clock continues forward and a few people come in the diner and take a booth at the other end. The man at the counter gets up to leave. Adin catches his eye, and rather than look away he holds the man's stare. Then the man pulls his coat on and heads out into the pouring rain. He wonders about the dark cloud.

"He could be dead within a year," Lairlux says softly, her gaze following the man as well.

"What do you mean?"

"What you saw is the mark of death," she says. "Think of it like the potential for death. He is clinically depressed and will take his own life within a year if he does not get help."

Adin blinks in surprise. Not only that she could discern all that, but that every day she must see that kind of thing around her all the time. He shakes his head in realization, feeling a newfound awe and respect for his friend.

"Do you help them when you see that?" he asks.

Lairlux's expression is sad. "I try. The witch in me feels obligated. So I try," she says. She does not say if has ever succeeded. She does not say how hard it is to do. She doesn't have to. Adin can see the difficulty of it in her expression, the uncharacteristic sadness in her eyes. They lapse into silence sipping their coffee and tuning out the inane chatter of the group at the far end. Their waitress moves with efficiency, keeping up with the energetic group. The spark he saw in her makes him wonder.

"Are all werewolves purple?" he asks suddenly.

Lairlux lets out a short laugh. "Only two that I've met," she says with a chuckle. "Have you met your mate?"

The question catches him off guard. "I'm wondering if I ever will," he answers honestly. At twenty-six the possibility is becoming increasingly unlikely. "Is that what that means?"

Lairlux lifts a shoulder. "I'm not an expert in werewolf lore, but the only other werewolf I've met who's purple never mated."

Adin blinked. "Did they just not find their mate?"

She shrugs. "He did not exactly travel much," she says. "He was a recluse, only interacting with a few other werewolves." She gives a half smile and adds, "He always said his mate was his spirit guide."

Adin's expression turns skeptical. "His '*spirit guide*' was his mate?"

The demon-human hybrid waves it off. "There have been stranger matches."

A thought occurs to Adin then. "Do demons and witches have matches the same way werewolves do?"

That half smile grows a bit as she answers coyly, "Do you think my parents were a mate match?"

Adin doesn't answer. While that wasn't exactly the reason he asked, it is a fair question.

Lairlux's answer is interrupted by the arrival of their food. The waitress sets down their collection of plates, somehow managing to carry them all in one trip. She then pops back behind the counter and comes back to refill their coffee mugs and leave some steak sauce for Adin. When that is done, Adin and Lairlux fall into silence eating their various breakfast foods, the meal feeling comforting after the news they received earlier.

After a few minutes like that, Lairlux suddenly answers his

question. "So in a sense witches and demons can have mates. It's just not instinctual the way it is for weres." She shoves another bite of pancake in her mouth. She says around the pancake bite, "It's more of a soul or spirit thing. To be honest I don't understand it yet."

A few more minutes pass as Adin enjoys his steak and eggs. This diner always cooks the best food. He pushes his empty plate aside and picks at his pancakes between sips of coffee. He watches Lairlux finish her pancakes with relish. The two sit in companionable silence, watching the rain continue to pour down outside and the occasional arrival of a diner or two getting a late-night meal. The clock reads 10:47 on the wall. Their meeting was later than usual, but the bar doesn't really open till ten most nights. The unusual group remained inconspicuous.

"What bothers me," Lairlux says suddenly, "is how targeted the illness seems."

"You mean, it's too coincidental that mostly creatures are getting sick?"

She nods, her eyes still on the street outside. "That's what worries me."

"Who would kill creatures?"

"Who wouldn't?" she asks back, meeting his eyes. The red demon eyes hold his gaze, anger simmering just below the surface. Adin does not look away.

"Do you think they've considered this?"

The demon red doesn't fade. She raises and lowers a single shoulder. "Asa's reputation would suggest she has." Adin snorts. Asa is known for being a bit persnickety. It doesn't help that her mother is a retired hunter. Asa is the black sheep of the family for being a healer. If she had not been extraordinarily gifted at it, her family might not have supported her. Even so she can't completely escape the Shertz family's widely known reputation for hunting.

Adin shakes his head. "I don't know what to think," he says. "I don't think we've seen the last deaths." His stomach twists in knots thinking of Esyn and all the others vulnerable to the disease. At this point it feels like everyone could contract it.

This time Lairlux reaches out and clasps Adin's hand. The contact does not bring the visions it did before. She simply holds his hand for a few moments to provide comfort. Adin accepts it gratefully.

Eventually they let go of each other's hand. The waitress brings their check with a smile and a friendly attitude, likely having seen their closeness. Adin pays the bill at Lairlux's protest. And they step outside the diner, standing awkwardly on the sidewalk. The rain still pours down. Adin feels again that the dreariness fits his mood.

Without thinking he puts his arm around Lairlux and

begins walking in the direction of her apartment, feeling protective and suddenly afraid. *Afraid? Yes, afraid.* The value he places on the people around him, and especially on those he considers family, makes him afraid they could all be gone in an instant. All at the hands of a mysterious virus.

Lairlux wraps her arm around his waist and pulls closer to him. He meets her eyes and he sees it. That same fear looks back at him. Holding each other closely for comfort, they keep walking into the rainy night.

4

ISOLATION

Chloe's comically small SUV barely holds the three passengers and all their medical paraphernalia. At Asa's urging, she, Kai, and Oriphine decided to ride with her to the pack house. One of Asa's learned skills is teleportation, but it is taxing and not possible for her to transport more than just herself. Plus it would have been rude to transport them all there. Kai secretly did not want to piggyback with her as teleportation can make her sick to her stomach. So she sits happily wedged in the back seat, shoulder to shoulder with Oriphine.

In the close quarters she has finally gotten a real look at the spirit. Oriphine chose to look more feminine than masculine and asked that they refer to her that way. But an underlying androgenousness permeates her features. Her skin has a natural luminousness that makes the deep mocha bright and youthful despite her likely age of over a century. Kai has never had the nerve to ask her how old she is.

On Oriphine's other side, a large sealed case takes up the seat. The case contains a specialized hazmat suit and other medical paraphernalia that would make their job possible when they get there. She borrowed some sealed sample kits from her friend at the CDC. Greg Nixon might be a human and completely unaware of the nature of the disease, but he is a good epidemiologist whose focus is on saving lives. He had not hesitated to give her the materials when she told him she was going to see some cases in the DC area.

Chloe's pack makes their home base in rural Virginia, but close enough to the city that they had met there. Kai dislikes being up at 4:30a.m., especially after a ritual night, but there is not a lot she could do about it. They wanted to get to Esyn as quickly as possible. The health of the child came first in her mind.

"How long till we get there?" she asks Chloe. They had taken an exit off I-66 and headed southwest into the rural mountainous country.

"At least an hour," she answers.

"Does anyone mind if I nap?" Kai asks, mostly directing the question at Oriphine next to her.

Asa snorts. "I might do the same," she says. "Rituals ran too late last night."

The full moon peaked overnight and half the covens in the area were up late conducting rituals. Both Asa and Kai showed up for the group ride with large tumblers of coffee. The caffeine wasn't working well enough unfortunately.

"I don't mind if Oriphine doesn't," Chloe says with a chuckle.

"I do not mind," the spirit says. "You may use me as a pillow if you like."

Kai's eyebrows go up at her words. Oriphine shifts in her seat so her shoulder is turned toward Kai and they are not wedged side by side. One glance at Chloe shows that she's trying to keep from laughing. Kai rolls her eyes and accepts the offer. She leans into Oriphine's soft shoulder, the spirit putting an arm around her.

"Thank you," Kai whispers.

"You're welcome," she hears back as a chin rests on her head.

Almost immediately her body relaxes, only the seatbelt and the spirit holding her in place. Before long she has fallen deeply asleep.

The car slowing down wakes her up and she blinks at their

surroundings. They are in rural Virginia alright, the rolling hills and mountains around them peppered with farmhouses among the open fields. They pass a sign for a winery and another for a church. A turnoff takes them onto a long driveway flanked on either side by woods. The trees here are not particularly dense, but the pack does not do much training here. They have another large plot of land in the mountains less than an hour away. The area around the house used to be more secluded, but as people moved closer the pack adapted.

Chloe explains all this to them as they round the last turn on the rather long driveway and come into sight of the house. No gate blocks the drive, but Chloe points out the camera mounted on one of the trees. She waves at it and they keep driving forward at a slower pace. They come to the crest of a hill and the house comes into view.

Their pack house is not just one building, but several smaller ones as well. Chloe points to the barn and explains it's not actually a barn, but another living quarters disguised as a barn. A large garage has several apartments built above it for pack warriors to live in. The house itself is three stories with an attic and looks like it could have come from the pages of a magazine. Someone in the pack has started putting up decorations for fall even though it is still the middle of September. The thought that someone in this house is as much of a diehard fall fan as Kai is makes her smile.

Oriphine gives her a squeeze and unwraps her arm from around Kai's shoulders. Chloe pulls the car around the house to a gravel parking area between the garage and the back porch. Around the back of the house, Kai can see the two other guest houses that no doubt several pack members live in.

Two burly looking werewolves step off the back porch and approach Chloe's car. Chloe turns off the engine and says, "Don't get out just yet. I have to check us in with the guards." She gets out of the vehicle but leaves her door open so they can all hear what she says to the two werewolves.

"I have Asa Shertz, Kai Soriano, and Oriphine to see Alpha Margrave and the patients," she explains. "They should be on the approved visitors list."

The taller werewolf looks back at the porch and nods at a third still on the porch. The third clearly younger werewolf dashes inside the house and pops back out a few minutes later. He gives a thumbs up to the tall werewolf and Chloe.

"You can get out now," Chloe says.

Kai opens her car door and extracts herself from the small SUV. Oriphine follows her, stretching her long limbs after the long ride. Without hesitation Kai circles the car and begins pulling the heavy case out from the back seat. She is surprised when the tall werewolf places a hand on her shoulder and says, "Allow me to help you."

She steps aside and says, "I would appreciate that. Just be gentle."

"Always," he answers with a smile. The other werewolf helps Asa pull her ritual case and a smaller crate of more mundane medical equipment out of the trunk of the SUV.

Chloe shuts the side car door and hands the keys to the younger werewolf who grins excitedly. "Be gentle, Remus," she warns. He pouts but hops behind the driver's seat and starts the engine. Chloe rolls her eyes as he pulls the car over to the garages.

The tall werewolf gently sets down the case on the porch and stands up offering his elbow to Kai. "I'm Lovell," he says. "That's Lincoln, my partner."

Lincoln grunts and puts down Asa's ritual case. He bumps Kai's elbow but doesn't say anything. He heads into the house with Lovell shaking his head. "You'll have to forgive him," he says. "My partner is the strong and silent type."

Kai represses a smile and exchanges a look with Asa now standing next to her.

A tall female werewolf comes out of the house onto the porch. She stops and surveys the newcomers with an air of authority that immediately makes Kai think she is pack leadership. Chloe sees her and approaches her differentially. "Beta Darla," she says, "this is Asa Shertz, Dr. Kai Soriano, and Oriphine. Asa, Kai, Oriphine, this is Beta Darla

Wesselman."

Kai steps up on the porch and bumps elbows with Beta Wesselman as she says, "Call me Beta Darla, or just Darla, my mate is Beta Wesselman."

"Call me Kai," she says with a smile.

Oriphine comes up onto the porch to stand next to Kai and bumps elbows with Darla.

"Forgive me," Darla says, "I've never met a spirit before."

Kai's eyebrows go up in surprise. It's not unusual to at least meet a spirit here and there in the creature world. But Oriphine just chuckles.

"You have though," she says. She points at a particularly large oak tree at the edge of the parking area with its branches arching protectively towards the house. As Kai watches, the tree shivers slightly though there is no wind. For a brief moment she can swear the face and body of a woman becomes visible in the bark. Then as quickly as it appears, it is gone.

"I had no idea!" Darla says in surprise. She shakes her head.

Remus comes back out of the house. "Beta Darla," he says. "They're ready for the visitors."

Darla nods and says, "Thank you Remus. I'll take them down." She explains to Kai and Oriphine, "We've converted the second guest house to a mini hospital. The hospital wing in the main house did not provide enough isolation."

Kai nodded. She opens up the case to briefly check the

equipment before shutting it again. She takes a handle and Darla surprises her by taking the other one. They head towards the far guest house, a deceptively small building that Darla tells her has twenty beds in it during normal times. They have been able to create a makeshift ICU for the more critical patients, but the beds are filling quickly. Kai is surprised to find out that Esyn is not the only critical patient.

"The others hadn't gotten that bad when we sent Chloe up to the meeting," she explains. "Chloe was away for school in Charlottesville and we knew she hadn't had contact with the patients. That's why we sent her."

As they approach the front of the guest house, Kai studies the building's exterior and notes that all the windows are sealed off and the door has a sealed vestibule for them to step through. Someone took the time to rig up an isolation for the whole house, not just the individual beds.

"Over here, please," a voice calls out, the owner waving them to a pop up tent.

A werewolf in his late fifties stands with a hazmat suit pulled on up to his waist. The rest hangs behind him, the air unit sitting on a table in front of him. Under the suit he wears a long-sleeve athletic shirt, something Kai relates to as the suits tend to get hot. He is in good shape, clearly still training with the pack though he is old enough that his hair is completely gray. Kai sees the deep scar on his cheek and neck, an old injury framing and somehow missing the brown eye.

Behind him several other werewolves, likely medical professionals or healers, move around equipment and monitor displays on laptops. On one screen Kai sees a video feed of one of the patient wards, two werewolves in suits weaving between the beds and checking patient vitals. At the far end of the tent, two other werewolves are suiting up as well. Every person under that tent except the older werewolf is wearing a mask of some kind.

As they approach, two younger male werewolves come up and take the medical case from Asa who joins them at a table. She begins unloading the significant supply of antibiotics, antiviral medication, and IV solution onto the table. The werewolves pull on gloves and begin sorting the supplies. One of them calls over a physician's assistant, a female werewolf in her thirties who begins preparing doses of medication for the critical patients.

Kai opens up her large case and pulls out a smaller metal one which has a hermetic seal on it. Any fluid samples they collect from the patients will be shipped in that container to Atlanta. She also begins pulling her hazmat suit out of the case.

Darla introduces the older werewolf who beckoned them to a pop up tent. "This is Dr. Josiah Fredegund. He is our pack doctor and healer." She places a hand on Kai's shoulder and introduces her, "This is Dr. Kai Soriano. She is here to collect samples for the CDC and see if she can do anything to help." She gestures at Asa and adds, "Asa Shertz is an earth witch. She brought medical supplies for us." Oriphine walks up behind them. "And this is Oriphine, an earth nymph."

Oriphine offers her hand to the doctor who shakes it with wide eyes. "Forgive me," he says, "I've never met a spirit before."

Rather than explain about the tree nymph, Oriphine just smiles at him and says nothing.

"Alright," Dr. Fredegund says. "We need everyone to wear hazmat suits. Dr. Soriano, I see you brought yours." He looks at Oriphine. "Miss Oriphine, we know it doesn't affect spirits at this point, but I would feel better if you isolate yourself as well."

Kai pulls a suit out of her case. It's specialized to allow her magic to work through it but keep her isolated from any supernatural threats. She steps into the legs of the suit and when she looks up she sees Oriphine glowing subtly. The spirit looks at her hands deep in concentration, the color of the glow shifting to a more purple tone. Then golden rings form around her wrists and the purple glow becomes more muted. Kai recognizes the magic as a type of shield technique, but she had never seen it done that way before.

Darla has donned a medical mask and will remain outside to lower her chance of exposure and keep some of the

Swifttooth leadership intact. With both the Alpha and Luna compromised, the pack's safety and continued existence depends on the Betas and Gammas. She tells Kai quietly that she hasn't seen them face to face for almost a week now. The worry in her eyes tells her everything.

Asa continues getting medical supplies sorted with the other three professionals. She won't be going in with them. Her eyes meeting Kai's are also filled with concern. Through the witch's mind link she silently tells her, *We should have brought more supplies.* With their surroundings looking more and more like a make-shift triage unit, Kai feels inclined to agree.

With her and Dr. Fredegund fully suited up and Oriphine sufficiently shielded, she and Oriphine lift the case together and follow Dr. Fredegund into the airlock. A few moments later they enter the building.

5

90 TO 95%

The guest house, likely once a warm welcoming place, feels sterile and sad in a way. Wood paneling and hardwood floors are now draped with clear plastic tarp crunching under their feet as they walk. A set of double doors to their left is shut tight with the plastic covering the doors completely and a sign taped to it reading ISOLATION – EARLY CARE. The wide staircase ahead of them holds another sign with an arrow pointing upward indicating the ICU is up there. The saddest part about the signs is not that they are there. It is that they were clearly printed from a computer and taped up with masking tape in the kind of hurried way that suggested they were unprepared for this.

Beyond the stairs on the first level a door propped open shows a kitchen converted to a lab and medication storage room. As they stand there a female werewolf in a hazmat suit walks by the door, barely glancing at them as she heads in the general direction of the isolation ward.

At first Kai is impressed at the level of care taken with converting the building. Then she remembers that the entire Alpha's family is ill and the sudden outbreak in their pack triggered the need for creative medical techniques. It is fortunate that enough of them have medical training to be able to provide the care necessary. If the medical professionals start coming down with the illness, Kai wonders how long the pack will survive.

The door shuts behind them and they hear the airlock emptying. For a moment the three of them just stand there, then Kai picks up one side of her case and Oriphine takes the other.

"This way," Dr. Fredegund says, leading them up the main staircase.

On the second floor, signs point to wards at either ends of the upper hallway. Critical cases are being housed to the left, but the ICU is located to the right. They walk to the right, heading toward a door flanked on either side by closets labeled as "MEDICAL SUPPLIES" and "LINENS ETC." The door to the room bears another printed sign, also taped to plastic covering the door.

Dr. Fredegund opens the door revealing a large dormitory, allowing Oriphine and Kai to pass him. A room that once housed a dozen pack warriors presents a grim alternative. Now it is divided into eight tight spaces, each an isolation unit with a critically ill patient in it. Each bed is closely divided from another by what looks like a rolling whiteboard used in boardrooms or college classrooms. On each board Kai can see a scrawled sample of the patient's vitals and notes on their medication. One glance around tells her they were throwing everything they could at these patients, but nothing was making a dent so far.

Kai and Oriphine set the case down inside the door and a couple of nurses or orderlies approach in hazmat suits and begin to unload the various supplies Kai has brought with her. Her doubts about their helpfulness grow with the number of ventilators around the room. All eight patients are either on a ventilator borrowed from a hospital or, in the case of one of the patients, what looks like a veterinary surgical setup. As they stand there, the female werewolf from downstairs comes in behind them and one of the nurses in the room leaves. Even in so short a time they have a routine down to keep the patients monitored constantly.

At the far end of the room, a werewolf couple waits for them, each wearing N95 masks and gloves as they hover over one bed. As they draw closer, Kai makes out the small form of a child. Even through her suit Kai can clearly make out the sound of a ventilator whirring away. The male werewolf meets her eyes and she sees the desperation there, recognizing him even with the mask on. The juxtaposition of the slight size of the child contrasted with the oversized medical equipment would be comical if the situation weren't so grave. Kai glances up at the whiteboard and the information written there. "ESYN MARGRAVE."

Kai approaches Esyn's ventilator and her vitals monitors, checking the display with an expert eye. The young werewolf lies deep in a coma. The machine is doing all the work for her. Kai's stomach churns at the hopelessness of Esyn's case. If they cannot help her, then maybe her case can help others.

Kai steps to one side of the child's bed and Oriphine steps to the other. In her head she hears the spirit's inner voice.

Can you examine her internally? Oriphine asks.

Kai meets her eyes. *A virtual MRI is what I usually call it*, she answers. As a doctor in the human world, she is sometimes limited by the scope of the science. What she does to help her patients cannot cross boundaries that would reveal that she is more than a human. In her heart she wishes she could offer more comfort to the dying or more help to the injured. But in the end, though she cannot reveal to every human she is a witch, she does have skills she isn't always able to use.

Together, is all Oriphine says.

They each reach for a hand, Kai's still gloved and Oriphine's shielded. Their eyes meet again, the nymph's changing color subtly from their usual brown to gold. Kai arches her spirit toward the child, feeling contact with Oriphine in the process. The sounds of the room drop away, the quiet shuddering of Esyn's mother and the soft conversation between Alpha Margrave and Dr. Fredegund and the sounds of the machines all fall away. It's just Kai and Oriphine now.

Together they examine Esyn, paying special attention to the antibody response and the virus's supernatural component. Because there is a supernatural component, Kai realizes. She had doubted it till now. The internal monologue tells her Oriphine felt the same way. The nymph silently hoped the virus would be a biological agent only, something much easier to treat in the long run. Those hopes dashed, they continue to seek out the virus in the child hoping to understand.

Between herself and Oriphine, they examine Esyn's organs in great detail. Specifically, they want to see how her lungs are holding up with the artificial breathing. Kai doesn't like what she finds. And she realizes that Oriphine, despite being outside

46

of the virus's scope, is not just worried but frightened.

The room comes back into focus. Silence envelopes them. The Alpha and Luna have moved to the end of the ward where they remain sitting in chairs with stress and fear all over both of their faces. A different set of nurses weaves in between the beds on the other side of the room. At the far end, Kai realizes they are preparing a ninth bed for another critical patient. Dr. Fredegund finishes checking on a large male werewolf and comes to them.

Kai glances down at the oxygen display on her wrist. She went in with two hours of air and it is now down to fifteen minutes. They spent considerable time examining Esyn. Kai feels the fatigue of such a long session creeping into the edges of her. One glance at Oriphine and she sees the spirit does not have unlimited energy.

"Is it as we expected?" Dr. Fredegund asks softly.

Kai answers, "Yes. About ninety to ninety-five percent engineered virus with the remaining amount supernatural. I couldn't quite figure out what." She looks questioningly at Oriphine.

The spirit is deep in concentration. A long pause goes by before she answers.

"I'm not sure what it is," she starts, "but there's something almost familiar about the disease. It reminds me of something from a long time ago." She doesn't add anymore, but the concern is evident on her face.

"Did you have a way to treat it?" Dr. Fredegund asks the obvious question.

Oriphine looks up. "I'm not sure," she says. "I don't know the disease that well. By the time I was born it was almost eradicated. I do know someone much older than I who would have known those infected."

"Can they come examine Esyn?" Kai asks.

Oriphine makes eye-contact with her. "I will ask," she says. "I am sure he will."

A moment or two pass. Dr. Fredegund breaks the silence. "We should get you two out of here and to guest quarters. If you wish to examine the rest of the critical patients, you can do so after resting."

Kai nods and says, "Let me take some samples from Esyn and that will be all for now." Dr. Fredegund nods in assent.

Rather than take the samples herself, Oriphine expertly draws the child's blood and takes a few nasal swabs as well. Then they seal their sample case and lock it. It will be overnight shipped to Atlanta. Hopefully Greg Nixon can give them some insight.

As they pass the Alpha and Luna on the way out, Kai can offer no words of hope and cannot even give them physical comfort. As much as she would like to hug the grieving mother, it would make leaving the isolation ward much more difficult. Instead she offers her assurances that they will do everything they can.

As she turns to take the stairs behind Oriphine and Dr. Fredegund, she looks back through the open door to the ward. The Luna hunches over, sobbing into her mate's arms. Kai's heart breaks knowing they are preparing to lose their only child.

6

ORDINARY EVERYTHING

The routine remains the same. Roland wakes up. He gets in a quick workout in his building's small but adequate gym. He goes back up to his apartment and showers. He walks a block to the nearest rail station. The light rail trains aren't the fastest in the world, but they offer an efficient means of getting around.

He takes the train, sometimes transferring twice, and most times stopping downtown at his favorite chain coffee shop. There is one near his apartment building, but Roland rarely stops there. Their training directs them not to make an impression near their homes or in their neighborhoods or really anywhere. So he always orders his coffee through a mobile app. Always places the order through a dummy account on a burner phone. Always uses a different gift card to pay until it runs out and he buys another one. Then he gets back on the train, drinks his favorite espresso drink, and finishes his trip to the outlying regions of the city. Once there, he hops off the train and takes three buses in a roundabout fashion to a building only a quarter mile from the station.

Every employee does something similar, taking routes HR has mapped out and at some point changed throughout the year. By the time he gets to work, often more than two hours after he leaves home, he has left an unintelligible trail of transfers and stops that would confuse most passersby.

The building he enters bears a simple logo, a stylized letter Z and three wavy lines meant to represent wind. They pose as an alternative energy company, with a public website and mission objectives that match. Several floors are even research labs for things like wind and solar energy. But if you look closer at the labs, they are merely window dressing for the biomedical labs further in the building.

Roland walks through the front vestibule and heads to the security gates before the elevator. He pulls out his keycard and swipes it. The lax-looking security guards drinking coffee and talking genially barely do more than nod and wave. What most people wouldn't notice is the tension in their postures, the casual way each of them at one point places a hand on their gun holster, the furtive glances at the employees gradually filtering into the building.

Roland stands at the elevator bank, a couple other employees joining him. He does not recognize any of them and does not try to remember faces anyway. He may have ridden with them a dozen times before and just would not know it. The elevator dings and he boards, hitting the number six before stepping to the back. A few other buttons light up and he waits for the long climb up to his floor.

After the other people have gotten off on lower floors and he is alone, the elevator dings again and lets him off on six. Beyond the elevator a much more robust and alert group of security guards waits for him. The nearly-empty vestibule flanked with white walls and white floor and white ceiling contains only a security station and a series of checks before the doors to the laboratory hallway. He steps forward to their station, a single guard directing him to place his thumb on the fingerprint reader and look into the retinal scanner. Roland has done this hundreds of times before, but the routine has never become normal. They always ask. He always does it.

A bright light, a faint sizzle on his skin and he is cleared.

He steps forward to the body scanner and the x-ray machine. He sets his bag down on the x-ray machine conveyor belt, glancing at the screen long enough to see his peanut butter and jelly sandwich get scanned deep in his lunch sack. The light on the body scanner goes green and he steps out.

A younger security guard hands him his bag and he silently takes it, heading for the door. Another scanner registers his thumb, the door lock buzzes, and he opens it and steps through. On the other side, another guard carrying a compact machine gun sits in a high top chair next to a rather normal looking secretary at her desk. She nods at Roland and greets him with a smile. The guard changes regularly, but only about a half dozen are assigned to the interior space. So Roland knows the man with his military build and ex-marine demeanor. He knows nothing about him, not even his name. None of the guards has a name-plate, just an ID number on their shirts.

The hallway is flanked on either side by that same bullet-proof glass that surrounds the conference room and the lab and the isolation biounit he primarily works in. A second layer to each of the floor-to-ceiling panes is smart glass that can change to opaque with the flip of a switch. One room he walks by is opaque so he is surprised when the door opens and his colleague calls out to him.

"Can we borrow you for a moment?" Kathryn asks.

"Sure," he answers, stepping into the room. Beyond is an ordinary meeting room, a smaller one than they were using a few weeks ago. At the table he recognizes a few other geneticists from their lab and the one adjoining theirs. On the projector screen a model of the latest protein scan rotates slowly, showing the three-dimensional structure. Roland sets his bag down on a glass table by the door and takes a seat at the table.

"This is the latest scan for group five," Kathryn says. "Can you take a look and tell me what you see?"

Roland studies the image for a few minutes, mentally inverting the protein upside down how he's used to looking at it. The bottom would be attached to the outer cell wall and the upward spike provides a connection point for the viral envelope to connect. The envelope would typically merge with the cell wall dumping the virus's genetic material inside. This protein is not like any he has looked at before.

"I don't see anything similar to groups one or three, so I think we should rule them out. The first few viral variants would probably not help us much here," he says. "May I?" he asks his colleague who graciously offers up the tablet they use to control the display. He taps it a few times and pulls up the protein located on group four, displaying them side-by-side. The two shapes are so dissimilar that even the amorphous three-dimensional structure is enough to spot the differences. He wipes group four from the screen and brings up group two on a long shot. There, a tiny similarity stands out to him.

"Do you see sub-A and its lower components?" he asks.

Kathryn nods, her poker face giving nothing away.

"It almost looks like this is a version of group two, but drastically altered," he says. "Do you think this might be the origin of group five? Or the other way around?"

Group five represents the one group untouched thus far by the virus. While it is possible the virus would naturally mutate to cover groups five and six, they were impatient enough to want to create one. Additionally, if they created it, the likelihood of the variant attacking plain humans would be lessened.

"We're not sure," Kathryn answers. "Getting samples from group five has been difficult, as you well know."

Difficult is an understatement. While he knew nothing of the strike team's inner workings, he had heard enough through the grapevine that several people had died along the way getting samples. Even worse, it seemed the best way to get samples was to send unwitting bystanders into the hornet's nest, so to speak, and let them get killed. The samples, as a result, are considered extremely valuable and kept under such a layer of security only a few people in the lab have access to them.

"The other part looks new," he says. He zooms the display in on a section labeled sub-H, the latest in a string of protein subcomponents they had discovered and subsequently labeled. "We might be able to work with this," he adds. "The end part looks oddly like group two which I would not have thought possible."

"I doubt either group would believe it possible either," she says dryly. "Then again the genetic similarities between those two groups really lends credence to the mythology."

Roland shrugs. "I would have thought there would be more similarity to group three."

A chuckle runs around the group. "I think we all would have," one of the others says.

"Alright, we needed the confirmation of an unbiased opinion," Kathryn says with a brief smile at Roland. "I think we'll do as you suggested and attack it from the angle of group two and see if we can figure out the unique proteins on it. Maybe it will give us a way to go after group five also."

Roland nods, silently setting aside his concerns that they would never get a group five subject to test it on. He hands the tablet back and picks up his coffee. He grabs his bag on the way out and heads further down the hall to his office. He shuts the door, the ambient sounds of the hallway and neighboring labs muted behind the double-paned glass. A flick of switch on the wall turns on the smart glass and blocks him from view.

He sinks into his chair, dropping his bag next to him. Unlike his house, which is practically sterile, his office is where the clutter is. Several piles occupy his desk and the table behind him. Everything is glass or polycarbonate except his black desk chair and his computer resting in front of him. Even working here for as long as he has, the complete lack of privacy sometimes bothers him. Sometimes he wishes he has an ordinary job, an ordinary career, an ordinary social life, just an ordinary everything. That ship sailed more than a decade ago. He would never get that life back.

Roland flicks on his computer, takes a look at the stack of files next to him, shuffling them and glancing briefly at the latest project he is working on with Kathryn. Group five's details are in that file, sparse though they may be. His screen lights up and he scans his thumb to log in.

Immediately an internal message pops up on the screen from their leader. The message is short to the point of terse, but she keeps her words to a minimum especially in writing. Attached is a spreadsheet Roland requested, a compiled file of the full groups with their details. No one but the leadership team has all the details about the groups. Part of him is stunned they are trusting him with this much information.

He scans the sheet taking it in quickly then begins to study it in more detail. The row labels indicate the group traits such as genetic markers, phenotype identifiers, number of samples collected, and it went on. The columns were new. Yes, they read groups one through five, but that wasn't all. Below them there were the common species names. And there weren't just five groups. Group zero started the pack, the moniker simply indicating human. Beyond five were a group six and a group seven, neither of which had a species name. Group six was marked as hybrid, but group seven piqued his interest by being marked as emergent. Could another species be on the rise?

He reads the names again: *human, witch, werewolf, demon, spirit, vampire, hybrid, emergent.*

Roland leans back in his chair, looking up at the blank ceiling. His DNA contains group two markers, a fact that unsettled him at first. A few generations back there was a single werewolf in his family line, something that bothers him as he was adopted. He never encountered a werewolf until he worked here. And when he did, it unsettled him. Finding out that myth and legend are real turned his life upside down. Finding out he was somehow a part of it brought everything in his world into question.

Even now Roland feels uncertainty at their progress, their goals, their objectives. He wouldn't say he regrets making the virus. No, he wouldn't say that. He regrets more not understanding how closely tied to humans the species had become to be hidden over the years. If the disease mutated enough, they could be responsible for a global pandemic.

He lets out a tight breath and takes another drink of his coffee. Setting aside his qualms and his fears for possibilities that haven't happened yet, he turns back to the chart and his work. He takes a post-it note and a sharpie and writes out a question, the next question their research must probe.

"*How do you kill a species that is virtually immortal?*"

He gets to work.

7

APPETITE FOR ALL THINGS GRUESOME

Half of the North American Vampire Royal Family is away for the week, deep in the wooded areas of the Northwest Territories hunting or the like. Only the King, his sister, the youngest Prince, and a couple of cousins are present at the table, a scant percentage of the usual bustling crowd. For once Nicolette is glad of their absence rather than rueful at being left behind. If what the witch's envoy says is true, their presence would only put them at risk.

My thoughts exactly, the Princess's voice floats in the back of her mind. She glances over at her cousin sitting at the table to the right of her. Nicolette's place is along the wall of the conference room.

A stray thought makes her mouth twitch in amusement. The whole idea of the North American Vampire Royal Family holding court in a large conference room dressed in normal everyday business suits never fits with anyone's idea of what vampires are. But that is exactly how they do their business. Some of the old positions in the court have been done away with or rolled into one position as technology and modernization made it possible. One thing that would never go away is the presence of lady's maids, valets, and the King's court at the far end of the conference room. Nicolette acts as Princess Irina's lady's maid and personal assistant and even envoy if necessary.

Shh, I'm trying to concentrate, the Princess scolds her in the back of her mind.

As one of the only telepaths in the vampire Royal Family and certainly the only other in this room, Princess Irina enjoys flexing her abilities as often as possible. Fortunately, Nicolette is one of the other few telepaths, not because it is an incidence of her vampiric abilities, but because she is half witch.

"We are not sure how quickly it will spread in vampires," Agatha Rex continues explaining. Her report has been appallingly bleak. The virus has spread to four continents. The clusters popping up in Asia and Europe have contained cases in almost every species. Two vampires in the European Royal Court showed signs of infection a few days ago. It spread rapidly enough that they were concerned the entire royal family would die out before the end of the year.

Agatha wears a mask sitting across from them. None of the court is wearing them now, but Nicolette feels that will change. As the thought crosses her mind, a young valet to the King opens the main door to the conference room and holds it open for an even younger valet who carries a dozen boxes of medical grade masks. They set them down on the table near the King's man who immediately opens a box of solid black masks. The two young valets take boxes and walk around the room handing them out.

Nicolette takes one with some relief and puts it on, setting down her iPad on the chair next to her for a moment. The screen shows the viral research she had pulled up, an unpublished article on the arXiv website detailing the latest sequencing done at the CDC. News of the virus had spread into the human media. While the existence of creatures is not widespread, there was no reason to prevent the knowledge of the virus from going public.

King Erasmus glances at the vampire to his left. Archduke Cyran Marcellus Lennix acts as both personal guard to the Royal Family and also as the COO of the business side of things. Cyran leans over and whispers in the King's ear for a moment. The King nods and whispers back. Even the vampires in the room cannot hear what is said. The King's ability to conceal vocals has long been his biggest asset.

"Madame Rex, I would like to send an envoy down to the group in the States," he says. "I think the Prince and Duchess Nicolette would be the appropriate choices given their backgrounds and abilities."

Nicolette sits up straighter in surprise, exchanging a look first with Princess Irina and then with Prince Ezra. The King is right of course. Prince Ezra has been a doctor for centuries and possesses a minor healing power, not quite on the level of a witch but good enough. Nicolette, as a blood witch, is well versed in the healing of both witches and vampires, no doubt a skill that would become invaluable in the next few months.

I'm a little stunned, Nicolette says.

Don't be, Princess Irina answers. *He knows the worth of those around him.* Her words reassure Nicolette that it is not a mistake after all.

"I will also send Cyran with them for protective purposes," the King continues, unaware of the silent conversation.

Cyran nods in agreement, no doubt glad of the assignment. In centuries past he had been everything from a Templar Knight to an explorer on the high seas to a fighter on the Pacific front in World War II. The desk job did not exactly jive with his personality, but he treats it like any other assignment and approaches it with military efficiency. The world is just different now and doesn't have space for crusaders.

While the King discusses his plans with Agatha Rex, she types away furiously at her phone and then pauses when he finishes. After a few moments, the answer comes back. She looks up and says, "My counterpart in Atlanta will be happy to work with you. She recommends meeting her at the Swifttooth pack house in Virginia first. She will be there for another few days administering to the Alpha's daughter."

A murmur of surprise runs through the room. Not only is it unusual for a vampire to visit a werewolf packhouse, it is flat-out bizarre to be *invited* to a packhouse.

Agatha's eyebrows go up at the murmur before she says, "These are unusual times."

You could say that again, the Princess says.

"I think we can finish there. Duchess Nicolette, Prince Ezra, please prepare to travel. I will have Cyran make the travel arrangements for you all," the King says. To Agatha he adds, "I trust you can help Cyran with a contact and a meeting location?"

Agatha nods.

"Alright, it's settled then." The King stands, causing the whole room to rise with him. "My family and trusted support, we'll leave it there. Spread the word of the necessary precautions. And do be safe everyone."

The King leads his court out of the conference room. Nicolette is one of the last to leave following Princess Irina, who is the King's niece. She acts as a treasurer to the Royal Family, answering to her mother the CFO. Just outside the door the Princess's mother and her lady's maid wait for them.

"Will you and Nicolette join me for a moment, daughter?" she asks. Princess Philomena Tereza Ursulette D'Arcy is not one to argue with. She is the most formidable member of the D'Arcy Royal Family, and one even the King occasionally answers to.

"Of course, mother," Princess Irina answers. She follows her mother down the hall and into the elevator, up several floors to one of the penthouses the Royal Family lives in currently. They never stay in a location longer than about a decade, or else their agelessness might be noticed.

The elevator opens up to the penthouse view of Lake Ontario to the south and Toronto to the north. The impeccably decorated space features barely-used furniture and a myriad of luxuries to make the most wealthy billionaire jealous. The Royal Family boasts an accumulated wealth well into the hundred trillions, but it is neatly divided amongst enough family members and corporate holdings to make them appear only barely billionaires. It makes it less obvious they have generations of wealth going back a millennium or, in the case of the King, nearly two millennia.

A lower vampire staff member, likely a housemaid or similar, brings a set of cups and several snacks out to a small table near the spectacular view. This is one of Nicolette's favorite things about being Princess Irina's lady's maid. Seeing these corners of Pier 27 and the luxuries her family's relatively minor duchy position could not afford them are the perks of being the Princess's closest ally and friend.

The four of them remove the masks as they take their places around the table. Princess Philomena herself pours cups of what smells like a fine bone broth seasoned with thyme and rosemary, the perfect warm drink for a vampire. She graciously hands a cup to her daughter, her maid, and Nicolette in turn, following the somewhat archaic traditions of nearly two centuries ago. Philomena is well over a millennium and she carries with her the memories of past times and past habits. Nicolette's light touch on her mind— a power that never really rests— gives her the impression of someone who has settled and been steadied by the passage of time. The world moves but the Princess is the stationary point in that motion.

After serving up the carefully prepared snacks, the maid retreats to give them privacy and Princess Mena takes her seat. Nicolette feels oddly claustrophobic with Philomena's maid on her left, the Princess on her right, and Philomena's scrutinizing stare across from her.

Archduchess Morwenna, Princess Philomena's maid,

genteelly passes a small plate of steak tartar niblets to her and Nicolette tries her best to use her finest manners. Her much younger age makes her feel like a child in this room and the insecurity makes her clumsy.

"My daughter, I would like to speak openly with your maid if you have no objection," Philomena starts.

Princess Irina raises her eyebrows. "Of course mother, if Nicolette has no objection."

"None, your majesty," Nicolette says to Princess Philomena.

The elder Princess offers a wry smile. "You may call me Mena, or ma'am if you must," she says. "I can't bear those titles all the time. In the court, sure, but not here in my own home."

Nicolette purses her lips. "Forgive me, ma'am. It's intimidating being a full three centuries the youngest in this room."

Princess Mena's features soften with understanding. "I understand dear, but really we are distant family. Your father's father was a good friend before he fell in the dark ages." The death she mentions is one not often spoken of in Nicolette's family, as it was painful for her family to lose the then patriarch. He was a beloved and prominent figure in the vampire community.

"Yes, ma'am." She pauses before asking, "What is it you

would like to say to me?"

Princess Mena's eyes shift to Princess Irina before she shakes her head. "I often forget your abilities mirror Irina's," she says with a laugh. "I only desire to ask you about your work. I want to know what you think about this virus."

Nicolette nods in understanding. Before she leaves for the States and takes her expertise with her, Princess Mena wants to pick her brain about the pandemic running through the creature world. She needs to know how serious to take it and the kind of measures she should take.

"I think we should take this as a threat to our person," Nicolette says, using the phrase tantamount to a declaration of war. "From what Agatha Rex says, the virus shows signs of being genetically created to kill creatures. Not all, not yet anyway. Up until a week ago there were no vampire cases, for example." She lets out a tight breath. "I'm not Cyran, I don't have a background in espionage and war. But if I were to guess, my instinct is telling me whoever created this will not be satisfied until all creatures are wiped from the face of the earth."

Her words fall into silence. Tension fills the room and Nicolette nervously lifts her teacup of bone broth and takes a sip. The hot liquid provides fortification against the chill in her core. Something awful is coming, and she doesn't need to be a seer to know that.

Morwenna offers her a plate of spinach pastries and Nicolette lets out a laugh. "Ah yes, pastries solve everything."

"They will at least solve your anxiety for the moment," she says with a wry smile. "How long since you satisfied the human food needs?"

Nicolette raises and lowers a shoulder. "Probably too long. The vampiric is much stronger." She takes a pastry and passes the plate to Princess Irina who takes one and hands it to her mother. These tiny delicacies are the perfect balance of non-vampiric junk food and fortifying spinach. The iron helps stabilize cravings for most vampires. As such iron supplements and iron-rich foods have become the fashion over the years.

Nicolette picks up her steak tartare, the delicacy losing its appeal in the current climate. The maid returns just then with the second round of snacks. Alongside the usual raw fish and other meats, a selection of actual human pastries and cucumber sandwiches are set aside on their own plate just for Nicolette. She takes the plate gratefully, feeling the nutrients are necessary for the ordeal to come. Normally vampires have an appetite for all things gruesome, but somehow this wasting disease, this attack of their perceived immortality and stable presences in the world, breaks that mold and turns her stomach.

Nicolette turns to the view and contemplates the time she

will spend away from her home. She truly doesn't know when she will return to the Royal House. Absently, she eats a cucumber sandwich feeling it might be the last sense of stability and calm she has for a long time.

8

DEFENSELESS AND FORGOTTEN

Adin holds Lairlux's hand as they walk down the long dusty old hallway of the underground space known simply as the Archive. The place itself doesn't unsettle him, the Archivist does. The creature leads them down this seemingly endless hallway tucked surreptitiously underneath a particle accelerator that oddly was once called "the world's most straight object." Indeed the room above them where the physics takes place spans a straight two mile length. Underneath, that corridor mirrors the central hallway of the creature Archives. Side hallways go further underground and hold every record imaginable, some going back to Mesopotamia.

"The Egyptians were, of course, the first Archivists," the demon Archivist continues his explanation as they walk. "Fortunately the main bulk of the Alexandria complex was copied and the originals taken out to Rome before the Great Library burned."

Adin raises his eyebrows as he looks at Lairlux. "The Library of Alexandria was a creature library?"

"Not entirely," the Archivist says with a wry smile that turns Adin's stomach. "But we certainly are the only ones who got records out."

Lairlux rolls her eyes. They continue walking down the corridor for what feels like another half hour. When Adin glances at his watch he realizes that his feeling is correct: it has indeed been another half hour.

"This way," the demon says, guiding them down a side hallway marked "Sp 001576-032949."

They walk down here for another half hour, taking three flights of stairs that lead them deeper and deeper underground. Every thirty feet or so a heavy metal door set into the thick walls bears a well-polished brass plate with a number on it. They pass what Adin counts as their fortieth door when the demon suddenly stops in front of the forty-second. The door reads "002819."

Rather than use a key, the Archivist presses his thumb against a completely ordinary part of the door. The metal hisses and a low "THUNK" resonates within the metal. A handle appears from the flat surface of the door and the Archivist opens it.

"Now, do not go wandering anywhere else," he says. "The Librarian will be by in about an hour to check on you. She will find you here and nowhere else." The warning in his words and the chill in his voice send a shiver up Adin's spine.

"Understood," Lairlux says with a touch of sarcasm in her voice.

With that the Archivist reaches through the doorway and presses a hand on the wall. Another lengthy room filled with a seemingly unending line of shelves lights up with old incandescent bulbs, except they're not electric. Even Adin without any magical ability can feel the fizzle of witchcraft in them.

"Good luck," the demon says with an equal touch of sarcasm in his voice. He turns on his heel and stalks away.

Adin lets out a tight breath and exchanges a hopeless look with Lairlux. "This seemed like a good idea," he mutters.

They walk into the room and stare at rows and rows of documents, scrolls, thick manuscripts with vellum pages, thinner hand-bound volumes clearly printed on old Gutenberg presses, and much else. Immediately in the entrance is a wide space devoid of anything but a table and a podium. On the podium, a single thick piece of vellum lays free of dust despite this place's age. Adin suddenly realizes the whole place is free of dust and the way he is able to identify the individual types of material in here is that they are nearly perfectly preserved.

"There's so much witchcraft in here," he whispers to Lairlux. It feels sacrilegious to speak loudly here.

Lairlux looks at him with a mixture of surprise and appreciation. They are still holding hands, but she lets go now. "Can you still sense it?" she asks quietly.

His eyebrows go up as he answers, "Yes." Confused, he asks, "What does that mean?"

"I'm not sure. And either way we should focus on this for now and think about that later."

"Fair enough." With another desperate look around, he asks, "Where should we start?"

Lairlux is the academic between the two of them. He went to community college and finished his AA, but he never finished his bachelor's degree. He doesn't really need it. Not for his job as a general all-around envoy with the pack. Sometimes he thinks he would benefit from international affairs training, but that is all he flirts with.

On the other hand, Lairlux is a brain. She completed an accelerated combined bachelor's and master's program in Chemistry, a branch of science that meshed well with her magical side. With a fire demon father and an air witch mother, understanding how combustion works in detail became her forte. She works now as a consultant for environmental firms and corporations that need their impact statements vetted for things like licensing and government contracts. In his mind Lairlux is one of the coolest people he knows.

A twitch of her mouth is all he needs to see to know she just read his mind.

"It's true," he whispers.

Her brown eyes flash red for a moment, but somehow that demon side of her does not feel scary anymore. With all the time they have been spending together, her darkness has become illuminated to him. She doesn't say anything else to him right then, however, and they move together to the podium in the middle of the room. He is both surprised and unsurprised to find the vellum blank.

"I have an idea how this place is cataloged," she says. She places a hand on the vellum and for a moment nothing happens. Then a single line of text—in *English* no less—appears in the center.

Welcome Lairlux Roseberg of the house of Chime and Kindra. You have been accepted.

"Do the same," Lairlux whispers, pulling her hand back.

Adin sets his hand on the page, wondering briefly what his will say. He was adopted into the pack as a child and never knew who his family was.

Welcome Adin Kennel of the Nightstar Pack. You have been accepted.

Deflated a tad, he pulls his hand back.

The page rewrites out the sentence, *State your desired search parameters.*

"We are looking for an incidence of disease that attacks creatures and humans with creature genes, please," Lairlux asks politely.

Approximate time frame?

"What did Kai text? What did Oriphine say?" she whispered to Adin.

He pulls out his phone, which naturally has barely any service. It doesn't matter. He opens up his texts and scrolls back through his exchange with Kai and finds the quote from Oriphine. The spirit had been born about three centuries after the last cases.

"Oriphine was born in the Sixth Dynasty of Egypt under Merenre Nemtyemsaf I. The last case would have been during the Fourth Dynasty under Djedefre."

Lairlux addresses the vellum, "Fourth Dynasty of Egypt and earlier, prior to the reign of Djedefre."

Searching.

After about fifteen minutes of the page repeating the word, Adin takes to pacing. After another ten minutes of doing that,

Lairlux walks up to him and pulls him into a hug. Their embraces had gotten more and more intimate since that night at the diner. In this moment, standing in this ancient Archive surrounded by layers of earth and the history of both their peoples, Adin lays his head on her shoulder and feels forever safe.

"It will be ok," she whispers.

He doesn't answer. The reassurance is enough even if he feels doubt underneath the comfort it gives him.

The vellum suddenly flashes a pale blue color. Together they step up to the podium and study the listings there. A series of books, a manuscript, and a plethora of scrolls form the bulk of the list. There is also an odd listing for a trunk as well.

Lairlux lets out a sigh. "I feel like my research life is never-ending," she says.

"Well I have practically no experience doing research, so I'll follow your lead," Adin answers. "Where should we start?"

Lairlux points to the five books on the list and says, "Why don't you go find those and I'll start pulling the scrolls? We can pull the manuscript later and find out what the deal with the trunk is when the Librarian gets here."

Adin lightly touches the numerals assigned to the books and the writing highlights in green. A tiny green ball of light pops out of the vellum and begins moving down the center aisle of the room. Adin follows it through a dozen stacks to a place where three book spines light up green as well. The magic in this room surpasses anything he had ever seen. Granted he hasn't seen much, but still.

With the five books in his arms, he walks back up the center aisle to join Lairlux at the podium. A cart has appeared out of nowhere and Lairlux has laid about a dozen scrolls out. She appears with another armful as Adin approaches the table and sets down the books.

Lairlux says to the air in general, "May we have chairs please?" and a couple chairs appear for them at the table.

Adin checks his watch then, seeing it has been just about an hour, and as if on cue the Librarian walks in. Neither he nor apparently Lairlux expected her to be a spirit and they both simply stand there staring. She looks them over appraisingly, inspecting the gathered paraphernalia in front of them. The spirit then walks over to the podium and glances down the list the vellum produced.

"You haven't pulled the trunk yet. Do you need help with it?" she asks in a musical voice. She is an earth-air spirit and Adin could hear the air influence in her voice. The earth part no doubt helps her stay underground comfortably.

"We would appreciate that," Lairlux answers. "I believe it is in another collection?"

"Yes, it is," the Librarian responds. "I will retrieve it and bring it back here for use. You will need to call me when you are finished so I can return it to its rightful place."

"Thank you," Adin says.

The Librarian nods and walks back out the door and down the hall in the direction going further underground. He turns his attention back to the thick volume he selected to start with. From his jacket, he pulls his tiny pocket notebook and a pen.

Lairlux looks up at his writing implements and snorts out a laugh. Rather than explain or say anything, she just reaches into the air next to her and pulls out a legal pad and a couple pens in black, blue, and red. She hands it all to Adin and shakes her head in amusement. Her own notebook is a classic black and white composition book that is half filled with notes from other things.

"Witches," Adin mutters playfully.

"Werewolves," she retorts with an exaggerated eye roll.

The Librarian returns just then with the trunk floating in mid air in front of her. She guides it to the center of the table which Adin and Lairlux hastily clear for her. "To be honest, I haven't looked in this for about six centuries," she says. The worn look of the case suggests that she was the last person to look at it as well.

Rather than have them open the case, the Librarian uses her abilities to open the case without touching it. She is either telekinetic or uses her air abilities to move things around, but it doesn't matter which. The case creaks open, but it is largely intact on the inside, clearly made of something sturdier than just wood and metal.

The trunk isn't what Adin would describe as ornate. Plain wood planks, uncarved and clearly aged, are bound together by metal strips. Inside the trunk, however, it is a different story altogether. Thin sheets of stone and metal make up what Adin presumes is a largely unbreakable chest. Within the chest are more parchments, but only about a half dozen, and a series of small glass apothecary jars each carefully sealed with a rubber stopper and a wax coating.

"I would not advise lifting those containers out," the Librarian says. "Those are the original samples of the disease you are looking for." She reaches in and carefully removes the small scrolls, setting them down before opening each in turn and laying them out flat on the tables. By some magic of hers probably, the scrolls stay open.

Etiquette would imply that neither Adin nor Lairlux touch the scrolls. So each leans over a scroll and copies down the writing. There are lines in Greek, Egyptian hieroglyphs, and something Adin assumes is Sumerian or similar. They would need help translating these documents to understand any of them.

"Would you be able to read these?" Adin asks the Librarian.

"Yes," she says, "but only the Greek and Egyptian. You'll need someone older to read the Sumerian. Someone who goes back at least to the first dynasty of Egypt, if you want the translation to be accurate," she adds.

Adin makes eye contact with Lairlux. She says what he is thinking. "I think Oriphine's older friend might be able to help with that." She turns to the Librarian and hands her her notebook with three scrolls worth of words on them. "Do you mind?"

The Librarian takes the notebook and her pen and sets it on the table. She sits for a moment reading before she begins her translation. Adin finishes copying his three scrolls and hands the legal pad to her as well. About ten minutes later they all look over the translations of the two known languages.

Among the descriptions of the disease and the spread, a phrase keeps repeating over and over. "*The Lost Ones.*" One section, an incomplete description in Egyptian, the Librarian has translated as, "*Lost Ones gone from Earth, took power and knowledge to death, killed with them the strength of old.*" After a lengthy paragraph in Sumerian, the last line in Greek says simply, "*Remember the Lost Ones lest they be forgotten. Lest we be defenseless and forgotten.*"

It's as if the air is sucked from the room. Adin looks over at both Lairlux and the Librarian. While the Librarian is neutral by requirement, even she looks alarmed.

"Who were the 'Lost Ones'?" Lairlux asks.

"The gods and the beasts of old," a voice says from the doorway.

Adin looks up to see the Archivist coming in toward them. He too looks concerned and his eyes going over the contents of the table show an unsettling anger. "I remember hearing of them when I was young," he says. "They all died out in a plague."

"Similar to now," Adin says.

"Similar to now," the Archivist repeats, his words causing the pit of Adin's stomach to drop.

Their fears were confirmed, as if they needed confirming. They were facing extinction. They were facing the end of all creatures. And if Asa and Kai and the CDC were correct, they were facing it within a year, maybe within months.

As one, all four creatures begin combing through the remaining scrolls and books. Adin finds himself studying in a way he never did in school, committing as much to memory as possible. Anger simmers just below the surface in all of them, an anger that propels them forward.

It is their own deaths they are seeking to prevent, as much as everyone else's. It is *all* their lives on the line.

9

A NYMPH WITH BROWN HAIR

Kai wakes up from a deep sleep with the scent of oranges and maple in her nose. For the second day in a row she looks up to see Oriphine's green eyes and cascade of brown hair looking at her. Rather than get up and face the trials of today like she knows she should, she sinks deeper into the nymph's arms and snuggles in the warmth for another few precious moments.

Never in a thousand years would she have expected an attraction to a nymph who had lived to see the Pharaohs. But that is exactly what happened. Kai falls in love easily, and she knows that and likes that about herself. She didn't expect one of those people to be this ethereal earth nymph with genteel manners and power she could never fathom.

Eventually Kai sits up and looks around them. Rather than spend last night in the guest house, the weather was nice enough outside that she did not object to spending the night among the leaves in the forest around the pack house. She runs her fingers through her hair and fishes out a couple leaves and some pine needles. She is studying the tangled ends of when Oriphine speaks.

"You're beautiful, even with tangled hair and leaves all over."

Kai laughs shortly. "Uh huh," she says. "You're a tad biased, aren't you?"

Oriphine grins, her whole face lighting up as she says, "Perhaps."

Kai leans over and kisses Oriphine before sighing and looking over towards the house. "We should head back and get ready. The vampire contingent is coming today," she says. A thought occurs to her. "Are you coming with us to Atlanta?"

Oriphine sits up and runs her fingers through Kai's hair. It immediately behaves and looks happier than it has in years. "I will come with you if you do not mind. I enjoy being around you and with this rising darkness . . ." She doesn't finish the thought. She doesn't need to.

Kai lets out a tight breath as she says, "I know." She slips her hand in Kai's as they stand up and head to the guest house. Kai needs to change her clothes. Oriphine's clothing is conjured and thus immediately changeable as needed, an ability Kai feels jealous over. Clothing has never been her thing. She wears what she feels comfortable in.

About twenty minutes later, after Kai has done her morning routine and is wearing clothes appropriate for wearing a hazmat suit over, they head down the outside stairs and make their way around the garage. The guesthouse is really a three car garage with three apartments over it. Darla has put her and Oriphine in the farther one with Asa in the middle apartment. Asa could have stayed in the apartment with them, but her rituals are solitary in nature. Out of respect it is better that she be on her own.

Asa meets them between the garage and the main house, a mask already covering half her face. Her eyes go to Kai and Oriphine's clasped hands and then back up to Kai's eyes, amusement present in her expression. She doesn't say anything however, keeping her thoughts to herself.

Instead, she says, "Shall we go meet the vampires?"

Kai's eyebrows go up. "Are they here already?"

"Arrived just about ten minutes ago. They caught an earlier flight than expected," she explained.

"Lead on."

They follow Asa up to the house and go inside to the

oversized dining room. The space has been turned into a headquarters of sorts. The walls are now covered with whiteboards and pinboards and even one smartboard from who knows where. The latest in the disease tracking blinks on a world map on the board, little red dots representing clusters of cases around the world. One large dot in Russia and another in Zimbabwe are particularly troublesome. Several medium dots in Chile, along the borders of Romania and Moldova, in Singapore, and in Seattle are showing growth rates that would put them past the two biggest clusters in a matter of days. It was almost like the virus's mutations were accelerating past the evolutionary potential.

As Kai and Oriphine enter the room, the whole room looks up to greet them, including the three vampires across from them. Beside them, a lone human reacts with recognition as much as Kai does.

"Greg?" she asks in surprise. "What are you doing here?"

"Ezra called me and asked me to come up," he says, gesturing to the vampire next to him. "I knew you were up here, so I figured I might as well."

She approaches him, confusion filling her face. "Do you know Ezra?" she asks.

"Only by reputation," he says, giving Kai a brief elbow bump. His eyes look around the room and the people in it who have gone back to working on the pandemic. "Listen, Kai, can we have a conversation somewhere?"

Darla, who walks into the room as he asks that, says, "Go out to the front porch. You can talk without being interrupted there."

Kai nods and says, "Follow me." She walks through the house like she lives there and leads him to the front door. She thinks she knows what this is about, but it's hard to say how much Greg picked up on.

On the front porch, they go to the far end, a single werewolf guard heading back inside to give them privacy. She sits on a cozy wicker bench and Greg sits on the matching chair next to her. Kai looks at him expectantly, waiting for him to say what's on his mind. She doesn't have to wait long.

"I have to ask you something, Kai, and I don't want you to take offense to what I'm about to ask." She nods, encouraging him to go on. "What exactly are you? I ran your DNA like I ran the rest. And you ping very strongly for one of the genetic markers the virus is targeting. So I have to ask you, what am I getting into here?" He gestures at the house with his last words.

Kai pauses. She knows she would have had this conversation with Greg eventually. She knows she trusts him enough to tell him who and what she is. She just never expected these to be the circumstances.

Just tell him, Oriphine says in the back of her mind. *He can handle it. And he already suspects.*

She takes a deep breath and braces herself. "Greg, I'm a witch." His eyebrows go up. "Most of the people in there are werewolves, but Ezra and his two colleagues are vampires. Oriphine, the woman I came in with, she is a spirit. Specifically an earth nymph. And Asa is a witch also." She stops there feeling she just dumped a lot of information on him. She lets Greg process what she said and fidgets impatiently waiting for him to do what she feels he's going to do—accept who and what they all are.

With his eyebrows knitted together, all he says is, "She's a nymph? I guess I always pictured them having blue hair and glowing skin or something. I never thought I'd see a nymph with brown hair."

Kai bursts out laughing. "See Greg? This is why I wanted to tell you," she says.

He looks up at her, pulled out of his thoughts. "You wanted to tell me?"

She smiles at him. "Well, yeah. I trust you. I didn't want this to be the circumstances, but I wanted to tell you because we're friends," she says. "And it's not like you don't have a power yourself," she adds with a wink.

Greg's eyebrows go up, his brown eyes sparkling at the remark. "You mean my synesthesia?"

"And your ADHD," she says. "Being neurodivergent is a

kind of power. You see things others can't. You feel things others don't. That's the definition of what it is to be a creature."

He is nodding, a smile slowly forming on his face. And then his eyebrows furrow. "You might be right, actually," he says. "I tested myself for the genes you and the others have, and I have one similar to the one you labeled S1."

Kai's jaw drops. She's utterly flummoxed. It's not that she's surprised he has the gene. Many humans likely have genes. It's the gene he has that surprises her.

"S1 is Oriphine's sample."

"You mean I'm part spirit?"

In the back of her mind, she can feel Oriphine coming out to the porch. She looks up as the spirit comes through the door and heads over to join them. She holds out a hand and Oriphine takes as she sits down next to her.

"Am I part spirit?" Greg asks his question again.

"No, but you have ancestry somewhere that was spirit or spirit-adjacent," Oriphine says. "Did any of your grandparents live to be over a hundred years old?"

He looks off into the distance thinking. After a moment he says, "I believe my mother's mother did. And I think my great-grandfather lived to be a hundred and six."

Oriphine nods. "It must be back there somewhere," she says. "But it could go back to ancient times, so it would be impossible to check the precise ancestry."

Greg nods, clearly still pondering the idea of being part spirit and having a power after all. Though it wasn't a true magical power, Kai still thought of it that way. When she saw patients diagnosed with it, she usually talked about it in terms like that. It always helps them reframe their diagnoses.

"Ezra is a vampire?" he asks.

"Yes."

"Ok." After a moment he stands up. "Let's go back into the war room. I want to get updated. I'll contemplate what all this means for my existence later."

Kai stands up too, Oriphine standing next to her. "Are we ok, Greg?"

The broad sparkling smile she has come to associate with her human friend lights up his whole face. "Of course we are." He looks at her slyly and says, "I always knew there was something different about you."

Oriphine leads them to the front door and goes through. Greg stops Kai for a moment and whispers, "And don't think you're going to get out of telling me what is going on between you and her."

Kai snorts in surprise. Greg is a worse gossip than most grandmothers. To hear him say something so completely normal caught her totally off guard. He must be taking the revelation as well as Oriphine said he would.

He is, she says silently. *And I'd like to have that conversation myself.*

She gulps as she follows Greg back into the house. He heads into the dining room, summoned by Ezra waving him over. Rather than go immediately back in, Kai stops Oriphine in the same way Greg stopped her.

You know what's going on, she says. *You know what I'm feeling for you.*

I am feeling it for you too, the spirit says, sending a wave of nervous energy through Kai's stomach.

She reaches out and takes her spirit's hand. Her spirit. Oriphine is Kai's spirit. The thought gives her joy in a way that her relationship with her last boyfriend didn't. She reaches up, lowers her mask with Oriphine doing the same. No one is around them at all, they are all in the dining room. She leans up and kisses Oriphine.

What was intended to be a single gentle peck became a life-altering passionate embrace. The spirit pulls her close, Kai pulling her in as well. The world turns upside-down for a moment, with her lips on the lips of this ancient spirit who has known more lifetimes than she can count. But for now, in this lifetime, they are each other's.

They pull back from each other, raise their masks. Kai blushes at the riskiness and blatant passion of it all. They take each other's hands and head back into the dining room.

The crew of creatures is working quietly when they come in. Then Asa says, "You're not supposed to take your masks off, you know."

Kai's eyes go so wide she is afraid they'll pop out of their sockets. She hears a camera on a phone click.

"Oh your face is priceless," Asa says. "Yes we saw you two."

Oriphine steps behind Kai and encircles her with her arms. She rests her chin on Kai's shoulder and says, "Well a ray of sunshine in a rainstorm should not be ignored."

"Well said," the female vampire says with a twinkle in her eyes. "I think you're adorable." She walks up and extends an elbow to Kai who bumps it back. "Nicolette Nyx-Trevil."

"Wait, the Trevil witches?" Kai says incredulously.

"Yes." If vampires could blush, this one certainly was.

"Kai Soriano," she says after a moment.

"I know who you are," she says. "If only by reputation, Doctor Soriano."

"Kai, please," she says. "And we can definitely use your help with Esyn."

"The Alpha's daughter?"

"Yes, we should have you examine her as well."

Nicolette turns back to the other vampires. "Prince Ezra, I am going to accompany Kai and Oriphine into isolation. I want to examine this child."

Ezra looks up from the viral genome sequencing reports he is reading. "Yes," he says. "I would like to go too, but you should be the first."

"When?" Nicolette says to Kai.

"Half an hour?" She turns to Greg. "You should come too."

He nods. Kai heads past him on the way to the back of the house and could swear she heard him mutter "vampire *prince*" to himself as he follows the group out back.

Kai smiles to herself, feeling that something is going right. Even if it is something small. Something personal. Even if it is only friends and new loves.

The feeling fades as they head to the isolation building. The building is filling at an alarming rate. Dread settles over her, wondering how much longer before they all need to be in a place like this.

10

DEMON IN A GRAVEYARD

Thelphise perches invisibly at the top of what would once have been called a tower. Now they call them skyscrapers and these are taller than any tower he knew in his youth. He enjoys high places and deep dark nights like this one. He remembers a time when night was truly dark, with no cities and no fires to light the night. When only your eyes could save you from being killed in the depths of the blackness.

Now light ranges freely throughout the world.

Part of him truly hates the way the world has become. He is a creature of the dark times, living in the era before the word civilization carried any meaning. He remembers the hunter-gatherer days, as humans tend to refer to them. Those days should really be called the death or survival era. He was a creature of the underworld long before the underworld became a thing of myth and legend. Now all that he is is a figment of people's imagination.

His cellphone rings.

Thelphise sighs in annoyance. Even figments have to adhere to modern conveniences to keep up with the times. He pulls the annoying contraption out of his jacket pocket and answers it.

"*What?!*"

"Is this Thelphise?"

He lets out a tight breath, trying really hard to hang onto the hair's breadth of patience he has tonight. "Yes," he says through gritted teeth.

"Are you a friend of Oriphine?"

Surprised now, his voice softens at the mention of Oriphine, his kind of daughter, kind of niece, kind of protégée. "I am. Who is this?" he asks.

"I am the demon Sorkelen. Oriphine asked me to get in touch with you," Sorkelen says on the other end. "Are you aware of the pandemic attacking creatures?"

Thelphise's eyebrows go up. "I had heard rumors, but I thought they were just rumors."

"Unfortunately, they're not," Sorkelen answers. "Can you meet us in an hour? I just texted you the location. It will be me and several others working on the case."

Thelphise checks his texts. He hesitates. It isn't that he isn't interested in meeting with the demon and trying to find out what is going on. It's that it just never seems wise to meet a demon in a graveyard. He is also in New York and the graveyard is in the DC metro area. So he isn't sure how he feels about teleporting that distance tonight. But he sighs, knowing he is going despite all his trepidation.

"I'll be there."

"Good. See you then." The demon hangs up without another word.

Thelphise turns off his screen and looks over the edge of the building. No one can see him up here, but he still watches his back anyway. He fixes his tie and adjusts his suit jacket. He wears the clothes of the period he is in. Even though his own time period was not so persnickety about clothing choices.

A moment of concentration and he puts himself on the ground. Over the centuries he has learned it is easier to transport at ground level to ground level. There's some calculus to it, something about it being one less variable to deal with. But really long before Newton and Leibnitz started that debate, he knew it on instinct alone.

Since he has an hour he pops around the corner to a local

cafe, part of him abhorring the chain cafes seen on every corner. This place he frequents enough that his occasionally disturbing spirit self is regarded as almost normal. Chelsea is on duty tonight as he orders his normal double espresso and a scone. He might be an underworld spirit but he still likes sweets. He just takes them with the bitterest coffee he can find.

The girl hands him a doppio cup on a tiny plate and sets a plate of scones next to it. The place is nearly empty, only a few people scattered around, so Chelsea takes the opportunity to catch up.

"Have you heard about this virus thing?" she asks.

"Yes, I just talked to someone about it," he answers.

"Scary how quickly it's spreading and how many people are dying."

He nods in agreement. The fact that humans are noticing a creature disease is concerning to say the least. Creature issues rarely make the news in the human world.

"Do you think Apexi is going to make any headway?' she asks.

"What?"

"The medical company working on a treatment."

This is news to him. "I didn't know anyone was working on one."

She nods. "It was on the news earlier. They're trying to find a treatment and a vaccine for it."

The company name rings a bell but he can't say why. He brushes that thought aside for now.

"Here's hoping they make a breakthrough soon," he says.

"Yes," Chelsea says. "That all you need?"

"That's all, I have to get somewhere in about thirty minutes," Thelphise says. He reaches into his pocket and sets a five dollar bill on the table.

"Alright," Chelsea answers. "Well you be careful out there."

"Will do."

Thelphise leaves the cafe and heads down the street. He's always been careful about where he teleports from and this is no exception. He steps into an alley unnoticed by anyone around him. He makes himself invisible again and then stands in an alley doorway. The door across from him opens as he teleports out.

Thelphise reappears an instant later surrounded by gravestones. He is alone for the moment but remains invisible, unsure who he is meeting. Saint Mary's Catholic Cemetery likely doesn't host many demons and spirits. But tonight there will be at least two.

About twenty feet from Thelphise, a demon pops into view, looking around him. Thelphise waits a minute to give him time, then makes himself visible. The demon sees him and waves awkwardly. Thelphise heads toward the demon, skirting headstones and graves to avoid walking over the resting.

"Thelphise?" the demon asks.

"Yes," he says. "Sorkelen?"

The demon nods. "My colleague may join us, but he hasn't confirmed yet."

Thelphise nods, grateful for the warning that another demon might be showing up. "So what did Oriphine need?" he asks, making it clear he is here for her and her alone.

"I was asked to meet with you on her behalf. She is with Kai Soriano at one of the packhouses out in the country," he explains. "They got word from Adin Kennel and Lairlux Roseburg at the Archives. They need help translating some Sumerian text they found. It relates to the ongoing pandemic."

Thelphise's eyebrows go up. He takes out his cellphone for a moment and glances through his texts. He has a couple missed calls from Oriphine, but she did not leave a voicemail. She must not have felt safe leaving the message. As any demon or spirit knows, technology is about as stable as human governments. Everything can be corrupted given enough time.

"Where should I meet them?" he asks.

"San Francisco, at the SLAC accelerator, but I'm sure you know where the Archives are," Sorkelen adds. "They are there with the Librarian and the Archivist continuing to dig through the material on the Lost Ones."

The phrase takes Thelphise aback. He cannot remember

the last time he heard the phrase in relation to a disease. "Do you think this might be some form of the old plague?" he asks.

Sorkelen raises and lowers a shoulder. "I don't know. I'm on the team trying to figure out who created the virus in the first place," he says. "But we're not having much luck. Hopefully the research at the Archives will help."

A pop sound signals another teleporter has shown up. Thelphise turns, expecting a demon, and is surprised to find Nyxie, a spirit he knows, standing there.

"Sorkelen," she says and then sees Thelphise and squeaks out his name in surprise. Of all the spirits he knows, she is the only one truly capable of passing for human, largely because she has a drop of human blood from the ancient times. Her father's father's mother was human.

"Are you on the, uh, spy team as well?" Thelphise asks.

Nyxie lets out a bark of a laugh. "I guess you could call us that. I'm here just reporting back because I won't get a chance for at least a few days."

"Don't let me hold you up," he says cordially.

Nyxie turns to Sorkelen and says, "I took a job with a pharmaceutical company under the pseudonym Caitlin Lawson. I'll be working with them starting on Monday. I'll keep you posted. The only thing we know for sure is that people who tie back to their company traveled to all the locations where the outbreaks started."

Sorkelen nods. "We confirmed it with our contacts at the FAA," he says. "We pulled the manifests and you were all correct."

Nyxie lets out a breath. "Good," she says. "That means we're on the right track."

"Is it Apexi?" Thelphise asks.

"Oh no, not at all," she answers. "Apexi caters mostly to creatures. Some of the medical and healing creatures are helping them work on a cure or a vaccine of some kind."

Thelphise nods. That explains why the company name stuck out to him earlier.

"We're investigating Zeusair at the moment," she adds.

"Alright well, be careful and keep us posted," Sorkelen says.

Nyxie nods, gives a brief farewell to Thelphise, and disappears just like that. No doubt she is concerned about being under surveillance at home now that she's dipping her toe into the world of spies.

"Is there anything else?" Thelphise asks.

"Just one thing," the demon says. "Given that you're an underworld spirit, would you be able to help with the critically ill patients?"

"I don't see why not. I'm not sure how much help I can give, but I can at least take a look."

Thelphise has some medical background, but any training

he had is woefully out of date, by at least a hundred years. Leeches are not the norm anymore.

"I'll send you Oriphine's location, though she may be in Atlanta by the time you get there," he says. "They want to be sure the CDC has everything they can to try to solve this. No one wants to rely on the private sector."

"Just let them know I'll get there after working with the Archive team," he says. "And maybe put me in touch with someone there already."

Sorkelen nods. "Chloe Plank has been working as a liaison to outsider creatures at their packhouse. I'll connect you with her."

Sorkelen pulls out his phone and sends a series of texts that light up Thelphise's phone. Then the two lapse into awkward silence for a few minutes.

Thelphise says suddenly, "I will let you know when I'm done at the Archives. It will take me half the night to get to the west coast."

"Be careful," is all the demon says before teleporting out.

With raised eyebrows Thelphise does the same.

11

SCIENCE WITHOUT RESTRICTIONS

In the labs at the CDC, the atmosphere is warm even if the labs themselves are chilly. Nicolette wraps her lab coat around her tighter, wishing the nitrile gloves offered warmth as well as protection. She is currently only working with their own tissue samples and preparing them for work in the level four bio lab. Greg and Ezra's idea is to deliberately attack the vampire and spirit cells and see if they can find a weakness in the viral structure they can exploit. So this means preparing everything from blood to tissue to saliva samples. Fortunately she is not working alone on the project. At another lab hood,

Greg and Ezra chat amiably as they work on the tissues from Oriphine. Across the room Kai and the spirit sit working away at a high power modeling computer trying to make sense of the data they have so far.

The biggest problem is not having data from all the clusters. The huge clusters in Russia and Africa are by far the most troubling. And for sure some data from those regions would be helpful. But as there has not been enough sequencing done to understand why, in the case of Russia, only werewolves have been infected so far. Granted werewolves, or оборотень as they are known locally, make up the creature majority in that country. It just seemed odd that they would not have cases in the smaller but still prevalent vampire population yet. Even the witches seemed bypassed in that country thus far.

"Nicolette," a voice brings her out of her reverie. She looks up to meet Kai's gaze. "Do you have your and Ezra's cell samples ready?"

"Yes," she says, "Right here." She indicates the two test tubes of cell samples scraped from their inside cheeks and another two taken from samples of their muscles.

"Can you bring them over there?" she asks, indicating the main central incubator.

Nicolette carefully seals the test tubes and shuts the hood off. She lifts the plastic vials delicately and brings them across the room to the incubator. They were growing cell cultures from each of the species, all which were in that room. Then they would be brought into a level four biolab for exposure to the virus. Samples of the virus are under heavy lock and key at the CDC, like most viral samples.

Greg, that intrepid human who for some reason knew Ezra by name, steps away from his lab hood and says, "You can leave them there. I'd like to do the cultures myself."

"Are you sure?" she asks, setting the tubes in the incubator and shutting the door.

"Yeah, it's a persnickety scientist thing," he says, brushing off his obvious care and attention to his work. "Y'all can meet us in the break room on the fourth floor. This won't take long and I'm sure you want to get out of your PPE."

Kai laughs. "After spending a few days at the packhouse in full hazmat, I think this is not that bad," she says, referring to their masks, gloves, and goggles.

Still, each of them de-gloves, disposes of their masks, puts their goggles in the UV sterilizer, and proceeds to wash their hands thoroughly. Nicolette follows Kai and Oriphine out of the lab, each grabbing hand sanitizer by the door, and then heads up the stairwell to the next floor. The break room he spoke of is down a mezzanine open to the floor-to-ceiling windows on one wall. The three of them grab the cheap government coffee and take seats together.

Nicolette adjusts her visitor's badge on its metal chain and shifts in her seat. Even after so many centuries she is still not good at sitting still.

"Nicolette?" Kai asks her. Pulled out of her thoughts, she looks questioningly at the witch. "Can I ask you something?"

"Sure, anything," the vampire answers.

"Were you born a vampire or turned?"

The question makes Nicolette smile. "I was born a vampire," she answers. "My family is a cousin to the King. I actually hold the title of Duchess, but I don't use it outside of court."

"Oh, wow," Kai says.

"Yeah, most of the royal family and court are born vampires, with some exceptions," she says. "More exceptions these days than a hundred years ago though."

Kai grows thoughtful. "I was wondering how a born vampire's cells would react versus a turned vampire," she says with a gesture brushing off her words. "My mind wandered."

"It's not a bad thought," Nicolette answers, mulling it over. "My physiology would certainly be different from that of a turned vampire. Also, I am half witch, so that does make a difference."

Kai's eyebrows go up. "I didn't know that!" she says in surprise.

Nicolette laughs reflexively. "It's not exactly a secret," she says, embarrassed. For a vampire, she sure can blush. "I come from prestigious lines on each side. I just work for the vampire court, so that usually comes up first."

"How old are you?" Oriphine asks.

Knowing the spirit is ancient, likely back to ancient Egypt from the smell of her, Nicolette is not offended by the question. "I was born in 1799," she says, "In England actually. I moved to North America when my vampire family did. My mother's family is still mostly in England, but that is not surprising."

"Oh?" Kai prods.

Nicolette shifts in her seat. "Well . . . my mother's family transplanted from Russia during the revolution," she says. "They decided to stay there, but my mother moved with my father to Canada when his family made the move."

"Oh, and you are born from an immortal witch line?"

This makes her smile as well. Kai is sharp, a trait she appreciates in people. "Yes," she says. "The Trevils go back a long time. It was Medvedeva Georgievna who chose the surname of her best friend. We were not Trevils before then."

There are not many immortal witch lines left. The bloodlines gradually got diluted over time. There are certainly ways in which to kill an immortal witch, something the burnings proved. She rubs the NATB tattoo on her wrist reflexively thinking of the burnings. But really the demise of the lines came from time and lack of other immortal witches to have children with.

Kai shakes her head. "An old friend of mine is a Trevil. Sasha Trevil, to be precise. We were in school together," she says.

"Oh! That's my cousin. She lives in Moscow now."

"Small world," Kai says.

"You have no idea," Oriphine remarks with a chuckle. She gently places an arm around Kai, pulling the witch closer to her.

"So what kind of craft do you practice?" Kai asks Nicolette while leaning back into Oriphine's arm.

"Blood magic, of course," she says with a self-deprecating laugh. "I'm the only one in my family currently though, at least the only exclusive blood witch." She shrugs. "My one cousin dabbles, but she is a full witch and I have the vampire side as an advantage."

Greg and Ezra walk into the break area then, stopping at the beverage bar on the side of the room. Greg grabs coffee while Ezra gets tea. They join the group and take seats.

"Well that's ready," Greg says. "I took a sample of cells to the level four lab. They're in the incubator down there. Hopefully we'll grow some additional samples, but I'll keep you posted if we need more."

"Kai made a good point," Nicolette says. "The samples are

only from the two of us. We are both born vampires, and I'm half witch. You may want to get samples from a turned vampire as well."

Ezra elbows Greg and says playfully, "Would you like to be a vampire?" He waggles his eyebrows at him.

Greg rolls his eyes. "That is not a decision I can make right now."

Kai looks like she might burst out laughing but she holds it back. Instead she exchanges a knowing glance with both Oriphine and Nicolette and says, "Should we get lunch or go back to work?"

"Lunch," Nicolette says immediately. "Has Cyran found us a sushi place or should we take a recommendation from the variety club here?"

Ezra pulls out his phone and says to Greg, "He suggested this place called Thaicoon?"

"Oh yeah. It's right down the street," Greg says. "They're good. Do you eat sushi?" he adds to Ezra.

"I eat sashimi, yes. Just not a lot of rice," he answers.

"Alright, let's get some lunch and then come back and see if we can infect some cells," Greg says, rubbing his hands together in a comically devious way.

The group laughs and gets up to leave.

Dark thoughts circle Nicolette's mind. She was starving a moment ago, but she suddenly feels her stomach drop at

Greg's words. Something tells her it won't be long before all species will be at risk. Something tells her the pandemic is far from over.

12

GRANDE VANILLA AMERICANO, WITH CREAM

Roland has the same dream every night.

He runs as fast as he can through a building. It's a corporate type building where the hallways all look the same and everything is gray. Even the doors to the offices are flat gray. He keeps running, looking for a place to hide. He can't see the thing chasing him, just sense it coming. It doesn't move fast—it doesn't need to. It can catch him just by wearing him down.

Sometimes in the dream he hides. He goes into the janitor's closet and crouches down, holding his breath as the *thing* goes past outside. Does it go past? Or does it stop and smell him and tear open the door? He doesn't know. He just wakes up in a cold sweat, feeling like the dream is real and he is truly being chased.

This morning the thing almost catches him. He wakes up and looks at the clock. 4:53. He kicks off his sweat-soaked sheets and switches on a light. There is no point going back to sleep. He does not know why he has these dreams. Perhaps because he's afraid of being caught by the creatures they are trying to kill. Perhaps because he is afraid of doing something wrong and their leader eliminating him as a liability. He's not sure.

Roland knows sleep is impossible after those dreams. So he gets up and goes to his building's gym, finding it empty. He works out for about forty-five minutes before stopping and heading back upstairs. A little after seven-thirty he heads out the door, his commuter's bag over his shoulder and an extra coat over one arm. The air began getting cooler the past couple days and the weather forecast showed possible snow on his way home.

He takes his usual circuitous route to the Starbucks in downtown. He thinks everyone at the store thinks he works in the business district, but that is definitely not the case. He picks up his order, reading the tag for a moment to make sure he has the right one. "Grande vanilla americano, with cream."

He sips the drink standing on the curb beside the stop for the train.

Since it's a light rail system, the trains aren't as fast as other cities, but the rails can be set into the roads and worked around traffic. He knows at this hour he won't be waiting long.

It starts as a prickling feeling on the back of his neck.

He ignores the sensation as leftover creepiness from his dream. But the sensation doesn't go away. Instead of continuing to ignore it, Roland surreptitiously looks around him at the people waiting at the train station. There are easily over a dozen passengers waiting, most dressed in working clothes like he is. One woman looks like she is going to a job cleaning houses.

Then he feels it again, that prickling sensation, on his face as he looks in the direction of a man. The man catches his eye. Except he knows that is no man. He has done his gene sequencing a few times and he knows he is group two. His markers come entirely from that group. So if the person is what he thinks he is, that person must be a werewolf.

The man nods at him cordially. He is wearing a medical mask, a habit several of the commuters had started picking up with the rising news coverage of the virus. Roland deliberately doesn't wear one because he knows it unnerves people and he is already vaccinated anyway. He will likely need a second injection, but he is covered at least mostly at the moment.

Roland faces forward again, shaking off the creeped out feeling. It must be a coincidence, but he is surely going to add a leg to his route today. He takes out his phone and messages their HR contact. "*Running late. Crowded train.*" The second half is code for a creature near him.

The response comes back. "*No worries. Take your time. I can meet you at Aurora West so you don't have to walk in.*"

Roland replies, "*Thanks. That would be appreciated.*"

The train pulls up. Mentally, Roland is already mapping out his new transfers to get to Aurora West. The werewolf steps onto the train behind him. He scoots down the car to an open seat at the back. The werewolf is near enough that he can keep an eye on him. He angles his phone like he's reading something and casually sneaks a picture. If a creature is following him, he should know who they are.

He gets off at one station and makes a transfer, taking the next train down a bit. Then he hops off at Aurora west. The prickling at the back of his neck tells him the werewolf is following him still.

A beat up gray car waits for him at the sidewalk and he hops in the passenger seat to make it look like he just had a friend pick him up. The driver is one of the security guards dressed as a casual businessman.

"Did they follow you?"

"Yes, all the way to this stop. It could be coincidence but

I'd rather be safe," he says. He looks back out the car window the way he came to see the werewolf waiting on the edge of the sidewalk for a bus. The bus goes back to downtown Denver.

"Maybe not," the guard says. "He picked you up in downtown?"

"Yeah . . . ," Roland says slowly. "I got a picture of him when I was on the train."

The guard nods, maneuvering the car down the road and out of sight of the station. After a few blocks he turns around completely and heads in the direction of their office. When they get there, the guard drops him off and he is met by a group of three from HR and security. They escort him to a first floor office where he sets his drink and for-show commuter bag on a table and takes a seat across from them.

For the next hour he details his routine, everything including where he goes for coffee and his order to the people he sees regularly in his neighborhood. He knows what's coming, and rather than feel annoyed by the task, he feels relieved it's time to move on.

"We're going to move you down to Aurora, I think," the HR representative says. "I'm afraid when something like this happens, it's best to relocate." The apologetic tone softens Roland even further.

"It's alright," Roland says. "I'm used to it. With the gene, I stand out a bit more than most of the techs."

Her face shows her sympathy. "I'm glad you're amenable, but I am acknowledging that it's terrible moving around so much," she says. Roland nods, showing he understands. It honestly just comes with the job. "I'll have our movers help you pack. We can hopefully get you moved by the end of the week."

"As long as there is a gym," he says with a laugh.

"Oh there is. A good one," she says chuckling. "In the meantime, I'm going to have you meet with Psyche before going back. It's normal procedure when we have to uproot one of our people."

Roland is also familiar with this process. With that, he makes his way to the seventh floor where the psychologists and psychiatrists work. He taps on the door of the woman who sees him every time he needs to have a check.

"Come in Roland," she says.

He opens the door and takes a seat across from her.

"Tell me what's going on."

He sighs. He hesitates. Then he begins to tell her what is really going on. For the first time in more than a decade, he opens up. Whether it is wise to talk about this or not, he tells her everything.

13

SHARED GRIEF

Chloe Plank opens her phone to the group text with Kai, Oriphine, and the others from the meeting that night. She sighs heavily and does the thing she wished she didn't have to do. Pain tears through her as she types out, "*Esyn Margrave passed this morning.*"

She hits send and only a breath passes before her sobs continue. Rather than be where her grief would bother others, she is hiding behind the garage guest house, letting herself feel the pain. In a few minutes she would have to stand up and be strong again. Right now, she is only going to feel the grief.

Esyn was a fixture in the pack. A genuine leader in the making, even at seven. She would have been eight in another month. Seeing a child die from this disease changed the seriousness of the infection. And she probably wouldn't be the last death that day. Three pack warriors are so critically ill, she doubts they will make it past lunch.

Quiet sobs shudder through her body. She doesn't want to attract attention to her grief. She's not sure how much time passes before she dries her eyes one last time, pulls on the N95 mask and slides her goggles on. She stands up and dusts herself off before heading into the main house. Only a couple days ago did they begin requiring masks for all people coming and going to the pack houses. Even the vampires had worn them while they were still here.

A drawn and exhausted-looking Lovell stands on the porch stretching out, his mask hanging by an ear while he is outside. He sees Chloe coming and pulls it up and his goggles down. His eyes meet Chloe's, sees the grief there, and nods in answer. They merely bump elbows in acknowledgement of their shared grief, no other physical contact is wise or permitted at this time. She stands on the lowest step and watches the guest house entrance across the lawn. Josiah stands aside, no longer an attending physician but a grieving pack member. Two hazmat clad individuals wheel a too-small body bag in a hazmat containment unit out of the house. The body of Esyn gets placed carefully in a coroner's truck to be taken to the nearest isolation site available. They would normally take their dead to the county coroner's office, but this marks an unusual occasion.

Her phone buzzes in her hand, still on vibrate from earlier. She steps away from the house and looks at the screen before answering.

"Hey, Kai," she says, her voice gravelly and worn from crying.

"I'm so sorry, Chloe. Please pass along all our condolences to Esyn's family and the whole pack," she says before anything else. "Greg made arrangements to have her body routed here. We're hoping her death can help us find a cure."

A half smile crosses Chloe's face, an expression so misplaced in this moment. "I think they'd like something good to come from her death."

"Maybe something can," she says. "Please tell them we wish our progress had been faster to help Esyn. We are still no closer to a cure, but with her we might get there."

Chloe nods as if Kai can see her. Maybe she can, what with being a witch and all. "I'll tell them." That's all she says before she hangs up and lets another sob shudder through her. The tall, wide figure of Lovell stands in front of her suddenly. She looks up at him, her tears causing steam to fog up her goggles.

"Go run," he says softly. "That's where Lincoln is right

now. It helps."

Chloe nods. "I have to tell them . . ." she trails off.

"I heard it all. I'll go tell them now," he says. "Go run. I'll let them know where you've gone. Go to the lower pack woods. There shouldn't be anyone there now."

She nods, knowing that would be the one thing that could make her shake the grief and come back to herself enough to be useful. Her car is still parked where Remus left it, keys still in the center console and door still unlocked. She had left it there because she didn't think she was going to leave anytime soon. Her pack go bag still sits tucked away in the trunk for when she needs to run near the university.

She gets into the car and goes down the driveway. Instead of turning the way they had come in, she turns toward the mountains and the forested land the pack owns. They kept it wild and free from humans to assure there are no prying eyes.

Her drive takes about a half hour on the windy two-lane roads of the mountains. She gets to the dirt road turnoff and takes it. About a quarter mile in, she comes to the small hunting cabin used by the pack as a starting point for their runs. Chloe parks her car and brings her bag inside the house. Though it is midday, she has always been able to shift at will. This will be nothing but therapeutic for her.

On the back porch, she strips down to her skin and takes a few steps down the stairs, shifting as she goes. Her brown hair and mocha skin give way to deep chestnut fur and yellow eyes that see far sharper than her human ones ever will. Her size is not the biggest, not being from an Alpha line, but she is above average as werewolves go. She is bigger than most of the Omega males in the pack. She takes a few steps more and shakes out her fur. It is long now, getting shaggy in response to the weather. Her inner wolf is quiet today, though she prefers to communicate in feelings and images rather than words. Today the grief runs through them both and her wolf chooses to remain silent.

The cooling autumn air feels like a blessing from the goddess on her fur. She runs and runs until she comes to the edge of the property and turns around and runs along the perimeter. She goes on and on until she feels her own grief and her wolf's grief settling down. Nothing could make it abate completely. But at least she can live with it right now so she can get things done.

She walks naked and a little more tired up to the cabin. She can smell another person waiting on the other side, another wolf from her pack. Chloe picks up her clothes inside and puts them on, slipping into her shoes last. She left her pack in the car, so she uses a brush kept in the house to get the inevitable leaves out of her hair. She dons a mask and heads out the front door.

The other wolf waits by their car, giving Chloe space to get in her car and leave. Then they walk into the cabin, presumably to shake off that same weariness that had been settling on all of them. She pulls her car away from the cabin and heads back to the main road.

14

ANY LIVING CREATURES

"Ah-*CHOO!*"

"Bless you," Lairlux says.

Adin's mouth twitches as he keeps from laughing at the spirit who has been sneezing on and off since arriving at the Archives.

"There's no dust in here," the Librarian says, clearly concerned as she hands Thelphise a tissue.

"Thank you," he says stuffily. "It's not dust. I'm allergic to age."

"*Age?*" the Archivist says skeptically. "Wouldn't you be

allergic to yourself?"

Lairlux snorts.

Thelphise glares at him. "I'm allergic to old *things*. To the time built up in them," he grumbles. "There's a reason I wear modern clothes. Anything older than a few centuries makes me sneeze."

Lairlux grins and hands him a parchment. "Is this older than a few centuries?"

Thelphise answers by giving a spectacular sneeze. He sets the parchment down and takes another tissue.

"Keep the box," the Librarian says with a concerned look on her face. "Let's finish up here sooner rather than later."

In the space of a few days, they had gotten through the majority of the Sumerian they had found before. None of the disease references were helpful though. Adin feels a kind of urgent frustration at the lack of information. They began combing through anything medical from the era around the disease and had still been coming up short.

"Well this could be something," Thelphise says. "I found a reference to a disease wiping out a group of vampires about a hundred years earlier than the first plague references." He scribbles in English for a few minutes while they wait and read their own texts more. "All right, listen to this," he says.

"A pestilence of mind and body. Hot skin, air not good. Even blood drinkers suffer. No humans except blends. Drinking the blood of a pure

human prolongs life. All true shifters died. Only partials remain now.

"Find the cure in spirit magic. Until the spirits fail too. True cures not real. All creatures die if the mind is not saved."

A deafening silence meets Thelphise's word. Adin lets out a tight breath. No cure for the original disease. If this even is a variation on the original disease, the lack of a true cure is troubling.

"True shifters . . ." Lairlux trails off a haunted expression on her face.

Adin had heard stories of them growing up. But he had never thought true shifters were real. He always thought they were a bedtime story, made up heroes of the old days. A true shifter was not bound to one species or one shape. They could become anything, from human to a tree to any animal—any living creature.

"So they did exist," Adin murmurs, awed by the possibility.

"And this killed all of them," Thelphise says, looking up and shaking his head. He sneezes again and picks up another tissue.

They sit in silence absorbing the fact that an entire species was wiped out due to this disease so long ago. A legend was real after all. A shiver runs up Adin's spine as he realizes this could make them all legends and no longer real. Across the table Lairlux's expression says she realizes the same thing.

"Sorry, it says 'Find the cure in spirit magic'?" Lairlux asks

125

suddenly.

"To some degree. I'm not sure if 'cure' or 'treatment' is the right answer, but there is certainly something there." He reads back through the text, holding his nose with a tissue to keep from sneezing. "And 'spirit magic' is the best I can do. I think 'magic' might also be 'incantation' or 'enchantment'," he adds.

Lairlux takes out her phone and begins typing, presumably texting the group chat about their findings. She hits send and it only takes a moment for a reply to come. She says, "Kai wants to know if the document can be brought to Atlanta."

Adin looks at the Archivist and the Librarian who have locked eyes. They are clearly communicating silently with each other. And the exchange goes on for a few minutes with Adin, Lairlux, and Thelphise just awkwardly reading texts or ignoring the two.

The Librarian lets out a tight breath. "We've determined that given the direness of the situation, you can take the text to Atlanta, but only if one of us accompanies it."

Lairlux types quickly for a moment. She waits. Her screen lights up with the response. "Kai says they wouldn't expect anything less."

"I'll get the storage container," the Archivist says begrudgingly. "The Librarian will accompany you."

"I will stay here and continue research," Thelphise says to everyone's surprise.

"Are you sure?" the Librarian asks.

"Just leave the tissues," he says, sounding very stuffy.

She pushes the box across the table with a wry look.

"I'll go close out my other work and get what I need for travel," she says. She leaves the room, leaving Adin, Lairlux, and Thelphise with the texts.

"You two are going to Atlanta?" Thelphise asks.

"I think it would be best," Lairlux says. "I believe we can teleport though."

"The Librarian should be able to take you."

"How old are you anyway," Lairlux asks suddenly. Adin feels the question might be rude to ask. But then Thelphise answers the question.

"It's old enough that I remember humans before they were humans, if you understand that," he says.

"Like cro magnon days?"

"Something like that. We didn't look like you back then," he says. "We were more ethereal, less corporeal. I just choose to look human to blend in."

Lairlux nods and says, "Same."

Adin's mind flashes back to the diner and when Lairlux showed him her true face.

"Yes, you understand," Thelphise says with an expression like he is studying her true features. "In any case, it gives me the ability to have a life now when being ethereal would not.

We aren't treated as gods anymore and we don't get the luxury of lazy existence."

"Where do you live?" Adin asks genuinely curious.

"New York mostly. Easier to blend in. My home is long gone, like the true gods of old," he adds. "So I make due with an apartment in the east village."

"Your home?"

"The Underworld. Gone with the last of the old gods."

An uncomfortable silence meets his words. Adin cannot imagine losing his home much less going for millennia without it. Then again werewolves tend to cluster. Still. Every creature needs to be near other creatures sometimes. The power within connects them, makes them feel whole. Adin relates to that which is why he connects with creatures like Lairlux.

She meets his eyes from across the table. Her red demon eyes surface for a fraction of a second. Something in him responds, not fear but with passion. He reaches a hand toward hers and she takes it without hesitating.

Thelphise leans back in his chair and raises an eyebrow at Adin. "It's been a long time since I've been near a werewolf who imprinted on a non-wolf mate."

Adin grips Lairlux's hand.

"Is that what this is?" she asks.

"I think so," he says.

"Well this is different."

"I'll say," the Librarian says from the doorway. "I totally called it. Your scents have been intermixed since you got here."

The Archivist rolls his eyes. "She'll be gloating for a century." He sets a heavy wooden case down on the table. Carefully he places the parchment pages Thelphise has been reading into the box. Thelphise hands his translations over to Adin who lets go of Lairlux's hand to put them in a bag. They would be taking both to Atlanta of course.

The Librarian takes the now sealed box. "Is everyone ready?"

Adin and Lairlux stand up and join the Librarian. "Do we need to go up to the surface?"

"No need," she says. "Just each of you take hold of my arms and hold hands. Should be easy," she teases. To Lairlux she says, "Text them that we're coming and that we need an open space near Oriphine."

Lairlux does so. She says, "They need one minute." After a pause, a message comes through. "They're ready."

"Take hold," the Librarian says.

Adin grips Lairlux's hand in nervousness. He has never teleported before. She squeezes it back, comforting him. Then the Archives blink out of view. And a moment later a large open space with windows all on one side comes into view.

For a moment Adin is fine, taking in the breakroom they

popped into. Then everything goes dark.

He passes out feeling Lairlux and another set of arms catch him as he falls.

15

UNKNOWN PERSON

Asa Shertz keeps her hood pulled up against the drizzle and against prying eyes as she turns down the alleyway and proceeds directly to the door of Alchemist Brewing. She knocks once and is let in without a moment's hesitation. A demon she is unfamiliar with asks her to identify herself. She completes the familiar routine and steps through the heavy curtains and the door to the bar beyond. She is stunned to find it empty at one in the morning on a Saturday.

Behind the counter, the proprietor sets down the glass he is polishing and gestures for Asa to take a seat.

"It's so empty, Lussios," Asa remarks.

"Everyone is staying in because of the virus," he answers.

"Even Orguth?"

Lussios shakes his head, a dark look in his eyes over his black mask. "Orguth is sick," he says. "And it doesn't look good."

Asa sinks into her chair with a feeling of despair. She had just come back from the Swifttooth pack and rather than quarantine she is here, waiting to gather information from a contact. They are desperate. Her N95 mask doesn't even feel like it is doing enough to protect her. Nothing does. Not even her magic.

Lussios taps the glass in front of her. A pale greenish brown liquid appears, steaming slightly. "Jasmine tea," he explains. "You look like you need it."

She nods. "I should keep my mask on."

"Fair enough." After a pause, "Do you want to go into the back room for your meeting?"

She shrugs. "Is there much chance of us being overheard tonight?"

"No."

"Then I'll stay here," she says.

The door opens and closes behind her. She turns in her chair and half waves at the woman who nods back and heads to the bar. Her black hair is pulled back in a messy bun, her clothes slightly disheveled business attire. She sits down at the bar and Lussios places a glass of pure human blood in front of her. The vampire shakes her head. "No, do you have spirit blood?"

He nods. "Do you want the bottle? No one else will touch it," he explains.

"They will soon." She doesn't remove her black mask, but Asa can see the bands from a second mask underneath. "They tried to infect me," she says. "I don't think it worked. But you should keep your distance."

Lussios nods and backs away to where Asa is sitting, some six stools down.

The vampire pulls a plastic bag out of her pocket and sets it on the bar. It contains a black and red usb drive and what looks like a couple spots of blood. "This is everything I could get," she says. "Hopefully it will be helpful." The bottle of spirit blood slides down the bar toward her. She takes it and stands up. "I heard this helps."

"It at least delays the illness," Asa says.

"Can't hurt, right?" the vampire says. She heads for the door. When she gets there she stops and turns back. "Oh I forgot. Behind all this there's some unknown person. When you find that person, I want an ounce of their blood."

Asa doesn't ask what she wants with the blood. She learned years ago not to ask. Instead she just nods and says, "I'll see what I can do."

The vampire doesn't answer, just leaves.

Asa just stares at the shut door for a moment. Then she snaps out of it and pulls a laptop from her bag. She floats the bag with the usb drive and Lussios takes out the antiseptic spray—really just 140 proof alcohol from the brewing side of the company. He holds up the spray bottle and mists the bag, using his magic to cover every nook and cranny of the plastic. Then when Asa opens it and floats out the usb drive, he further sterilizes it, careful not to get it too wet. The vodka would not have much effect on it, but just to be safe he doesn't overdo it. The bag Asa shuts and floats into another bag used for evidence collection. She closes it, intending to test the blood later. Then she takes the usb drive out of the air and plugs it into her computer.

Lussios proceeds to spray down the bar, the seat, and the general air path the vampire took through the place. Asa's mouth twitches in amusement as he waves the spray bottle through the air like he is conducting the symphony orchestra. Her computer dings, drawing her attention back to the matter at hand.

"What the . . . ?" she says, swearing as she reads file headers the vampire brought her.

Apexi Medical repeats over and over and over, in file after file. Her stomach drops and her heart starts racing. She lets out another swear, reading the first document. Line after line lists creature name after creature name, their "classification" denoting what kind of creature, and their susceptibility to the disease.

"Those . . ." Lussios calls the people who work for Apexi names that would make a grown sailor blush. "I'm with the vampire on this one. What is her name?"

"I don't know," Asa says. "She wanted to stay anonymous and I didn't push it."

"Ah," Lussios says. "I take it she is a spy."

"The credentials she gave me would suggest so, yes," she says. "I also had the American Vampire Regime check her out and she is legit. They wouldn't say who she works for, but she is one of them."

"Hm," he says. Reading over her shoulder he adds, "I suppose it is only a matter of time before all the species are infected then."

"That's what I'm afraid of," Asa says. "Plus this is interesting to me." She points to the listing for group seven and the word *emergent* next to it. "What could this mean?"

"A new species?" Lussios asks. "I'm not a scientist, but I imagine that's possible."

"Distinct from the hybrid's too," she says. Asa shakes her head. "I don't even know what to think," she says. She picks up her phone and texts the group chat with the information.

She also opens an email and attaches a zip file of documents to it. She types only "FYI" in the message and puts in the emails of the group at the CDC. She would join them, but her work with the Swifttooth pack would not be done anytime soon.

The door opens behind them and Lussios waves at the person who comes in. Clearly someone Lussios knows. She can hear the person coming in, but Asa's concentration is on the email. She hits send.

The hairs on the back of her neck stand up. She sits bolt upright on her stool and slaps the laptop shut. A spell radiates from her hand, binding it to her touch.

Lussios falls to the ground next to her.

One look at him and she knows he's dead.

"I wish you hadn't done that," the person says.

She looks them in the eye. "*YOU*," she says. "But *why*?"

"It doesn't matter to you."

Her heart stops.

The pain is incredible. She grabs her chest and drops to the ground next to Lussios. She has seconds and there's nothing she can do.

Her last sight is of the person taking her laptop and leaving the bar.

Her last thought is wondering who will take care of her plants.

16

NOT THE OFFENDER

The email sends a jolt of anxiety through Roland. Again he wonders if he needs to go on anti-anxiety medication, but they likely wouldn't be strong enough to cover all the problems he has. The subject of the email brings little relief. "*Security Breach*" glares at him. It isn't until he clicks on it that he feels relief. The breach has been resolved.

How in the world someone got into their database and managed to steal everything is beyond him. They erased some critical data as well, but not without a cost. He felt their security protocols, something he considered barbaric once, had done their job perfectly. The intruder was likely infected with the virus on their way out of the building. Unless the person belonged to group four or five, they would theoretically feel the effects of the illness before long.

His desk phone buzzes. He picks it up.

"Roland, come down to my office please," the voice says before she hangs up on him. It could only be one person.

He hangs up the phone and sighs. Roland takes a last sip of his coffee before heading down the hallway. Their leader's office is situated at the end of the hall on the corner. She keeps no secretary. The man who sits beside her in meetings is her deputy and his office is next to hers. Roland taps on the open door.

"Come in, Roland. And shut the door," she says firmly.

Uh oh. What did he do now?

He closes the door softly. The side door into the adjoining office opens, and the man who works with her steps through. "Ready?" he asks.

For the first time Roland really registers his appearance. He's definitely around Roland's age and has similar salt and pepper hair, likely also from stress. The difference is his icy blue eyes, not just icy from the color but also from the dead coldness there.

Roland takes the seat their leader offers, her partner taking a seat at the side of the room.

"Your position is such that we are raising your clearance level," she begins. "Do you understand what this means?"

Roland nods and says, "Yes."

"As I alerted you, we have neutralized the thief. What we were unwilling to put in writing is that we captured the thief late last night," she says. "We know you have been having difficulty getting samples from groups four and five. Not only is the specimen from group five, but they were carrying a bottle of group four blood."

Silence fills the room. Roland is stunned by this development. He had hoped to get his hands on a living group four individual, but a significant blood sample is more than he expected.

"Where is the specimen being held?" he asks.

"Level nine, high containment," she answers. "You will need this to get there." He takes the security badge she offers and clips it to his lanyard.

"You understand this is not something to be discussed among your colleagues," the man says. A cold look of warning fills his eyes. Roland would not want to run into him in a dark alley.

"I understand," he says, looking the man in the eye. Since moving and starting with the psychologist full-time, he has had much less patience for the intimidation around him. He does his job. Yes, he is scared of being discovered and of the creatures he is working so hard to destroy. But he is *not* the offender. The creatures are.

"Good," the woman says. Roland looks at her, fully memorizing her features. The scar on the back of her hand still remains the most notable thing about her. For the first time he wonders if a creature is responsible for the attack that caused the scar.

"Go up to the ninth floor. They are expecting you," she says.

With those words, he knows he is dismissed. Roland gets up and leaves the office, letting the door shut behind him. He looks down at the clearance tag and keeps walking down the hall. He goes through the security station, the guards nodding at him as if he leaves every day to go to a highly secured floor. Then again they aren't supposed to react to them at all, much less when they do something unusual like go to a secured floor.

On the ninth floor, he goes through another, heavier round of security and heads down a hallway distinctly different from his floor. The doors and walls are all solid, and clearly made of a heavy metal meant to withstand a lot of abuse. Indeed several bare dents from impacts to the interior of the door. He wonders what is in those holding cells. This place could only be a prison.

"Roland?" a voice asks. He turns and nods at the approaching man. "I am the curator here," he says by way of explanation. He extends his hand and Roland shakes it warily. No name, just a title of sorts. Roland feels uneven that his name is known to this stranger.

"I'm here to see the new one," he says.

"This way," the curator says. He leads him down the main hall and then to a narrower side hallway. At a doorway with no symbol but a plate with the number "7526" on it, the curator stops and taps on the door. A window opens in the metal and a pair of eyes sees who knocked, shuts the window, and opens the door for them to enter. The door shuts behind Roland and he takes a moment to adjust to the light.

Roland steps through unsure what he expected, but this is nothing like he had in mind. On the far side of the room behind what is presumably a wall of bulletproof glass, a woman with coal black hair and pale skin sits crouched, chained to the wall behind her. Her clothes are disheveled, but they likely once resembled a very passable business suit. Her wrists and skin burn where the metal touches them. Perhaps the allergy to silver is true.

"The cuffs are lined with mercury," the curator explains as if he could read Roland's thoughts. The vampire tugs on the chains at the sight of the newcomer and the two guards on either side of the door stiffen in response.

"She has broken the chains three times already," he says. "The mercury is the only thing seeming to work on her. She isn't reacting to the virus and we're not sure why."

"Is it the most recent strain?" Roland asks.

"No—," he begins.

"Let me out of here Roland Rommel," the vampire interrupts. Roland's head snaps around and he is looking at the vampire crouching, pulling on the chains. "I don't belong here and neither do you."

For a moment he feels doubt. He wonders if he should be doing what he does. He feels sympathy for the vampire crouched in front of him. Then he shakes it off, realizing the vampire is manipulating him.

Coldness touches his eyes and she screams at him pulling on the chains harder.

"Make sure she doesn't escape again. Even if you have to kill her," is all he says. "I can work with a dead specimen."

With that the curator leads him out of the room, the screams of the vampire following him the whole way.

17

SAMPLES OF THOSE GONE

At this point Thelphise should have adapted to the Archives, but his allergies are only worsening. He has resorted to taking Zyrtec, which feels ridiculous on its face. Why would a human medication ever offer relief to a spirit? But for some reason it's helping. And his face is only a little itchy and he is only sneezing a tiny bit.

"Do you think we'll find it?" he asks the Archivist. As a companion, the demon is not the most conversational. He does not mind that though.

The Archivist shrugs. "If we do, it will be here. Somewhere

in this room." He shivers. The room, he had admitted, gives him the creeps.

They are in the specimen repositorium from ancient days. What had been a quaint habit of collecting samples from unique members of the species had in modern days been considered a bizarre and taboo practice. The process had ended some five hundred years ago, but the collection had been preserved. When the Archives moved to San Francisco, it moved with the rest of the collection.

"Here," the Archivist says. "This is the oldest group we have. If there is a sample, it is here."

Daunted, Thelphise stares at the floor to ceiling chest of tiny drawers, each modern acrylic and backlit, holding some ancient alchemical vials with small samples of blood or preserved tissues. The idea of going through these hundreds of vials to look for the correct ones, or even ones that might come close, feels like it might take a year. And there's no telling if there are even samples of those gone among the collection.

"How do you want to divide this?" Thelphise asks.

"I'll start at the top. You start down here," he says. The Archivist goes down the row to grab a rolling ladder. For an ancient collection, it is certainly kept in very modern condition.

Thelphise rolls a cart over to the chest and begins extracting the bottom row of drawers. They are mostly small drawers, but there are large ones tucked between them here and there. One containing a five chambered heart stands out in his mind. The smell makes him wrinkle his nose. The formaldehyde wafts strongly every time he opens another drawer. He pulls a tissue out of his pocket and blows his nose.

The Archivist has pulled another cart over and is similarly emptying a row. He hands Thelphise a pair of gloves, indicating the box if he needs more, and then hands him a medical-grade mask. "Trust me," he says.

Thelphise puts the mask and gloves on. "Where should we put the samples we want to take?"

The Archivist pulls over a third cart and pats the top. "You'll have to teleport the whole cart with you when you take them."

"I can manage that."

"Well I hope so," he replies sarcastically.

Thelphise rolls his eyes and doesn't respond.

They lapse into silence working on the drawers and pulling sample after sample to transfer to Atlanta for testing. If they don't find the samples they are looking for, there is no telling how long it will take them to treat the disease. And this is all assuming the virus is anything like the old plague they keep reading about. The term plague doesn't bode well as it usually refers to a bacterial disease. But something about the broad nature of the translation makes Thelphise think it might have been a virus. They might have a chance here.

After what was likely an hour or longer, the Archivist suddenly says, "I think I found something."

Thelphise, half distracted by the tooth samples he is looking at, says, "Hm? What is it?"

The Archivist rolls over a microscope from the side chamber, the kind of microscope that is only found in the creature world. This kind of microscope can pick up on the slightest variations in cells that denote the presence of creature genes. DNA sequencing might be relatively new, but they had known for as long as humans have known about genetics that there are genetic markers to the creature species. Curiosity led to the kind of microscope now showing Thelphise the odd markers on the cell sample the Archivist noticed.

"Look at the intracellular proteins," he says.

Thelphise, leaning into the scope, adjusts the viewer slightly and says, "Huh. That's different."

The Archivist chuckles. "What do you think?" he says. "What we've been looking for?"

Thelphise straightens up and asks, "Do you have the record?" The Archivist hands it to him and reads the original notes on the sample. The date only goes back to the fall of the Roman Empire, but the ownership record is far more interesting. The collector, Caeso Novius Calatinus, noted the previous owners going back to the first collector of the sample. An Egyptian named Atemu had gotten the sample from a grave in a notably taboo way. He recorded the original sample as coming from a "lost one."

"I think we found what we're looking for," Thelphise says.

"Text them," the Archivist says. "They should get this sooner rather than later."

Thelphise nods and pulls his phone out. Miraculously he has service.

Several words later and a short exchange with the group chat and his jaw drops. He lets out a swear word.

"What happened?"

"Asa Shertz is dead. She's been murdered."

"The humans?"

"Someone who can use magic."

The Archivist draws a sharp breath. "Another creature?"

Thelphise shakes his head. "Someone is working with the humans."

They exchange a look. Both of them feel the same thing. How could a creature be so awful as to betray their own? How could they trust any of the others now?

18

EVERYONE HAS LIMITS

The shrill sound of his phone wakes Adin up in the early hours of morning. He untangles his arm from Lairlux, who stirs next to him. "What is it?" she murmurs, her grouchy demon side making the comment.

"Not sure," he says. He grabs his phone. Chloe Plank is calling him from Virginia.

"Chloe? What is it?" he asks.

"They found Asa Shertz's body yesterday," she says.

"*What?*" He and Lairlux both sit up in bed.

"Yes, she was murdered with magic," she says. "Whoever

it was stole her laptop."

Adin swears. "Is Kai ok? Does she know?"

There is a tense silence. "She's distraught. We're all blindsided by this, but they were friends." Chloe lets out a tense breath. "Can you pass along our condolences in person?"

"Of course," he says.

"And be careful," she says. "We have no idea who the traitor is."

She hangs up the phone leaving her last words echoing in Adin's head. Traitor. Whoever threw Asa under the bus certainly is a traitor.

His phone lights up. He has fourteen messages in the group chat. Everyone from Chloe to Thelphise is on this chat. The whole group is blowing up over Asa's death. She is the strongest healer witch of Adin's acquaintance, though he knows there are stronger healers. Her loss will be felt throughout the whole community.

"We should go in," he says. Lairlux gets out of bed and heads into the bathroom. For a moment Adin glimpses her red demon skin before she closes the door. He's learned that when she is stressed in any way the skin sometimes shows through. It explains the near eternal calm he always associated with her. It also explains why she meditates daily.

Adin gets up and gets dressed, waiting for Lairlux. When

she comes out of the bathroom, her eyes are red but from crying this time. Without thinking he puts his arms around her, pulls her into a hug, and just lets her cry. She is the strongest person he knows, but everyone has limits and everyone is allowed to cry. He knows she knew Asa, even if she wasn't as close to Asa as Kai was. He believes Asa might have been one of her mentors early on, when she was still figuring out what kind of witch she would turn out to be.

"I'm sorry," she croaks out between sobs. "I might be part demon, but murder is always shocking."

He rubs her back and whispers, "Don't apologize. You knew her far better than I did. I understand."

She nods, sniffling, and says, "You're going to have to change your shirt."

Adin lets out a bark of a laugh, a wry smile on his face. "I really don't mind. I kinda hate this shirt."

Lairlux laughs, the sound choked by tears and grief. She pulls back. "I'll get dressed and ready to go in. Does Greg know we're coming?"

"I'm sure he will shortly," Adin says. He glances at the clock. Even at four in the morning there are people who go into the CDC. So they would likely not stand out much from the crowd. Especially since they are all purportedly working on the new pandemic and there are cases as far away as Russia and South Asia.

His phone goes off again. A text from Greg reads, *I'll meet you all there in an hour.*

Relief floods Adin. The hour would give them time to get composed and find some coffee. He knew, to face this day, they would both need it.

"Where do you want to go?" Lairlux asks.

"Anywhere that is open."

She gives him a wry smile, her eyes still red-rimmed. "Another diner, perhaps? Or something similar?"

"How about Waffle House," he says, only half joking.

She rolls her eyes. "We can go to your first love." She comes over to him, dressed in jeans and a t-shirt, and puts her arms around Adin. Another sob comes unexpectedly. Fortunately Adin still needs to change his shirt.

He doesn't know how long he stands with her like that. He just knows he wants to have his arms around her for the rest of his life. He kisses the top of her head. Seeing her in grief like this upsets him. All he wants to do is soothe that pain. Deep inside, he suddenly knows he loves her.

She pulls back and looks up at him, no doubt following his thoughts. "I love you, too," she whispers. And the words are so strange coming from the half-demon that they are nothing but genuine.

Adin kisses her thoroughly before pulling away to change his shirt. So strange to feel the mixture of emotions, the deep love he has for Lairlux and the wrenching grief in the face of Asa's death. Somehow, Asa's death made it all the clearer.

Lairlux is his mate. He would do anything to protect her.

19

HOW THEY THINK

Nicolette sits in an unused corner of Greg Nixon's lab perched on a stool with a laptop open in front of her. It has taken her all night to crack the encryption on the files Asa sent right before her death. But Nicolette doesn't always need sleep and this is far more important than her REM cycle.

File after file lists Apexi Medical, and she for the life of her cannot imagine why they would be involved with this. So in the wee hours of the morning, long after the rest of the group left, she started tracking the finances of both companies to see what connection could exist. So far she struggled to find any.

As far as she could tell, Apexi Medical is completely ignorant of its assistance to Zeusair in creating the virus.

Something about it feels incredibly suspicious. The files sent over by Nyxie, what little she was able to smuggle out of Zeusair, provided no further insight and only confounded matters worse. No two companies existed the same between them. And what made things worse is she couldn't even find a connection on the medical research side where Zeusair would have taken in the medical samples from creatures. If they were working together, they were doing it so covertly that one branch had no idea what the other was doing. A classic case of the right hand not knowing what the left hand was doing.

She pushes back from the lab table, stretching her back as she stands up. Part of her is worn out so much that she can't even consider continuing to work. But part of her refuses to relent. Asa died to send this information out. She died to help them find a cure. The witch's efforts should be honored. The witch part of Nicolette refuses to ignore the significance of dying for a cause.

Her phone buzzes. She picks it up and is surprised to find a message from Cyran. The message reads, "*The American Court reports one of their spies has been missing for two days.*"

Confusion furrows her brow. Then a second message comes through. "*They suspect she is the source of Asa's information.*"

She swears out loud. Whoever got Asa could easily have gotten the missing spy. She texts back asking if they suspect as much.

"*Yes.*"

She swallows at the reply. Who is doing this? Who could be a traitor to their own kind? To creatures? It had to be a witch or hybrid witch who killed Asa. They could easily have incapacitated the missing vampire if she was caught unaware.

The door to the lab opens and Greg comes through. He gives a half wave to Nicolette, his face looking drawn and tired. The lower half is covered with a mask, as they had taken to wearing when around each other in the lab. Only once in a while, when they are alone in an isolated part of the facility, do any of them take them off for eating or drinking.

"How are you holding up?" Greg asks cordially. The human had taken to the creatures, especially Ezra, with a great deal of grace and acceptance. He had completely rewritten the narrative of humans for her.

"I hit a wall," she says. "Did you talk to Ezra?"

Greg nods. "The missing vampire?" When Nicolette nods back, he says, "Yeah. I suspect they might have taken her for samples." The look of horror on Nicolette's face makes him wince. "Sorry," he says. "I didn't mean to say that so bluntly."

"It's ok," she says. "I should have expected that." With a shake of her head, she adds, "If I try to think how they think,

I think that's how I would approach it."

Greg blinks at her. "'How they think,'" he repeats back. His face has gone vague and distant, a sign he is mulling over an idea that is consuming him. Frozen just inside the door still holding his backpack and coffee, he suddenly sets them down on a table and makes a beeline for the nearest research station. Curious, Nicolette gets up and peers over his shoulder.

On the screen, she sees the models of the various virus samples they had pulled, each with a protein that fits uniquely into the cell of a creature. She doesn't know what he is looking for. She is good with blood diseases, but this is beyond her. The nuances of virology escape her.

"I wonder," Greg murmurs. "I think I know what they're doing."

He doesn't elaborate. And Nicolette gets distracted by a text to her phone. "*We've found their headquarters. Your hunch is correct. They've been posing as Apexi Medical.*"

For a moment Nicolette just absorbs the information. Then she clenches her jaw in anger. So many creatures trust Apexi medical to help them with their specialized needs. They are run by creatures and thus are able to gain the trust of creatures. No vampire ever seeks for medical care. At least not outside of the vampire healers. Being half witch though, anger seethes in her realizing that the one time she went to Apexi and had blood drawn—she herself contributed to this.

Greg has been reading over her shoulder the whole time and his eyes are sympathetic. Early on he learned what Apexi really is to the creature community. "I'm so sorry," he says.

Nicolette nods. She bites her lip for a moment, then pulls up Ezra's number. To her cousin, the Prince of the Royal Court, she types, *I'm not taking no for an answer. I'm going to the lab with the team.* The message sends.

About two minutes later, the reply comes, "*Do what you need to do.*"

"Be careful," Greg says. He watches Nicolette as she walks out of the lab.

Down the hall, she steps into an elevator and heads to another floor, seeking the spirit Oriphine to help her teleport. The next message she sends is asking where the strike team is meeting. She would go directly there.

And she would not stop till she found out who or what took the missing vampire. And she would not be satisfied till she drank each of them dry.

20

CONTRASTS IN THE WORLD

Kai sits stony-faced in the break room, her phone forgotten in her hand. Next to her Oriphine rubs her back gently, feeling her grief and pain, helpless to do anything about it. Kai and Asa had worked together for so long. Asa had been a kind of mentor to Kai. That she was murdered sits far worse than if she had simply died. There is a hollowness where their friendship was.

"I want to go up to the coven and participate in the death ritual," she says suddenly.

"I can take us up there," Oriphine suggests.

"I'm not sure how wise it is to travel up there after being around all this."

Oriphine rubs her back more and murmurs, "Do you want to be cautious?"

Kai squeezes her eyes closed and leans forward, holding her head in her hands. "I don't want to be responsible for any illness they might get."

"What if I brought you to just watch and kept us shielded the whole time," Oriphine suggests.

"That might work," Kai says slowly. She hesitates to go because the entire coven comes from long lines of witches. Of all the people who would have genes making them susceptible to the disease, the entire coven represents that demographic.

"It's ok if you do not go," Oriphine whispers.

Kai nods her head, her eyes closed and tears slipping out. "I just don't know what to do."

"You don't have to make any decisions right now," Oriphine says. The spirit continues to rub her back, doing the best she can to comfort her witch. Kai knows this, and leans into Oriphine, letting the spirit's arm drape around her. She sets her phone down and puts her arms around Oriphine's waist. For the few moments she is in her embrace, she feels safe and at ease with the world.

"Even if you can't go to the death ritual, you can honor her in other ways," she says. "Honor her today by what we do to eliminate the enemy's threat."

Kai nods, feeling some relief at having a task. There is something to be said for keeping busy in a time of great stress.

"Oriphine," a voice calls. They both look up to see an intense-looking Nicolette heading towards them on a beeline. The breakroom, and really this whole floor, is deserted at this time of day. The only reason Kai and Oriphine are here this early is because Kai needed something to do. And then she felt paralyzed by grief and didn't quite make it to the lab.

"What's going on Nicolette?"

The vampire glances around, takes a seat opposite them, and lowers her voice. She says, "They found the lab. The strike team is going to go in sometime in the next twenty-four hours. I don't know when. I'm going to join them." The last line takes Kai by surprise. She hadn't pegged the vampire for a combatant.

"You need a way to get there," Oriphine says.

"Yes, if you don't mind."

"Of course."

The spirit slips her arm out from behind Kai. She then stands up and pulls out two of her hairs. Not fully corporeal, the hairs glimmer in the fluorescent lights. She ties the hairs around Nicolette's wrist where they glow brightly for a moment before becoming muted. They almost seem to sink into Nicolette's skin like some bizarre tattoo.

"Activate it by touching the hairs and thinking where you want to go." The vampire complies and appears on the other side of the room.

"Good," Oriphine remarks.

Nicolette returns to standing right next to her and says, "You heard about the missing vampire?" She is asking Kai as much as she is asking Oriphine.

Kai looks up at her with what she knows are red-rimmed eyes. "Yes," she croaks out. "Are you going to find her or avenge her?"

The glint in Nicolette's eye suggests the latter, but she says, "Both."

"Send them my regards," Kai says with heat in her voice. She stands up then and pulls the vampire into a hug, something Nicolette is clearly surprised by. They bear something of a kinship, given that they have witchblood in common between them. But otherwise Nicolette clearly leans more vampire than witch. She awkwardly wraps her arms around Kai and pats her back.

"I will," she says. "I'll make sure they get what's coming to them."

Kai nods as she pulls back and leans into Oriphine's embrace. "Be careful," she says almost reflexively.

The practically immortal vampire gives a wry smile. "Always," she says.

With that she disappears.

Kai faces Oriphine who smooths the hair over her ears. The spirit does not seem to know what to say. She is millennia old and Kai feels her sense of lostness at not knowing how to help her. She wraps her arms around the spirit, feeling again the bond between them. With everything horrible happening, the virus spreading practically unchecked, the disappearances and the murders, the death all around them. Kai holds in her arms the person keeping her going. The person she cares so much about, loves even. So she does the thing she had been wanting for a while but not quite gotten the courage to do.

She pulls back slightly and kisses Oriphine.

For just a moment, during their contact, she falls down into a world of beauty and ecstasy, a feeling of being in paradise and surrounded by joy. For a moment during that kiss, she knows real unadulterated bliss.

Then it's over and she's looking into the eyes of a very surprised ancient spirit. An ancient spirit who takes the opportunity to kiss her back.

Strange the juxtaposition of joy and endless grief. Strange the contrasts in the world.

21

LAUGHING AT THE END

Roland visits a coffee shop around the corner from his building most days of the week. It is the most innocuous, non-chain local establishment he could find. The coffee is not great. In fact it's so terrible that he has taken to just ordering regular coffee and not his usual drink. They never seem to get it right. He can't really complain. The benefit of living in the company building is he doesn't need to feel afraid of being spotted again.

Today he needs to run an extra errand after the coffee shop. So he takes his to-go coffee from the counter, for a moment feels a shiver he attributes to the door swinging open, and heads out of the shop with his mind on going to the bakery around the corner. Today is Kathryn's birthday and he means to pick up some cupcakes. Does this break the rules? Probably. But he doesn't care. He is loyal to the company and wants to show his intention to stay with the company for his career.

He walks into the bakery, the scent of fresh bread overwhelming him. The cupcakes display beckons and he finds himself feeling like a child with his nose pressed against the glass. Except he is wearing a mask and pressing his nose against the glass is probably below his dignity. Still, the cupcakes with the pink frosting are calling his name.

"Can I get you anything?" the lady asks from behind the counter.

"Yes," he says. "It's my coworker's birthday. I'd like a dozen cupcakes, please."

"Any in particular?"

"A couple of the pink ones for sure," he says.

The lady smiles as she says, "They are vanilla with strawberry frosting. Is that ok?"

"Yes," he says.

"Which other ones would you like?"

Roland takes a few minutes and picks out the remaining nine cupcakes—some chocolate, some vanilla, a couple other fun flavors. He doesn't know what anyone prefers, but that feels right for how little they talk to each other about themselves. Instead of worrying about it, he just picks what he thinks everyone will like.

"Anything else?" the lady asks.

"That'll do it."

Roland waits while she adds up his order and again asks if he doesn't want a croissant to go with his coffee. After hesitating, Roland assents finally. She pulls a fresh warm croissant from the shelf behind her, puts it in a pastry bag and tosses in a small to-go pack of Nutella. He hadn't had the stuff in years, but he does like it. Roland's sweet tooth is the reason he is so consistent with his workouts.

He tucks the pastry in his work bag and carefully lifts the box of cupcakes in his free hand.

"You got it?" she asks.

"I think so," he says, lofting it in a way to test the weight. "I think I got it."

She smiles broadly. "You'll be everyone's favorite today," she says. He smiles at the thought. A shiver goes up his spine as a customer comes in the door behind him. She wishes Roland a good day and turns to the newcomer.

The newcomer, seeing what Roland is carrying, holds the door for him. Roland thanks the person as he walks through, that shiver still traveling up his spine. He wishes he had a free hand to adjust his collar and keep the chill out. Ignoring the cold, he ducks through the door and heads down the street. The door shuts behind him.

Roland only has a few blocks till he has to turn off to head into the work campus. The building with the stylized Z looms ahead of him. A row of squat, worn buildings sit between him and the turnoff. The street feels deserted after the crowded walk to the coffee shop. He heads past the stores feeling oddly conspicuous with his box of cupcakes. He sips his coffee as he goes.

About two blocks from the turnoff, he starts to feel lightheaded. Attributing the feeling to the cold weather and his hunger, he keeps moving. The cupcakes suddenly feel heavy though, so he pauses next to a newspaper stand to set his coffee down and adjust the box. Then it occurs to him.

How did he know it was Kathryn's birthday if they never talk about personal details?

The chill runs up his spine again and he blinks. The feeling goes away. He lofts the box and picks up his coffee. He continues to walk down the sidewalk. The street is still deserted.

He takes no more than a dozen steps and feels lightheaded again. He looks down at the box, the realization hitting him again. How? How could he know?

He doesn't.

The cold seeps into his spine and up his neck. It sends a shiver and a spasm through his arm. He drops his coffee. The box tilts. He watches as the beautiful cupcakes fall to the ground in slow motion. Regret grips him as he watches them splatter, the box splitting open and spilling crumbs everywhere. He slowly sinks to his knees, his pants landing in the frosting on the ground.

He knows what is happening. He is powerless to stop it.

"He's fighting it," a voice whispers.

"He's going to be covered in sugar," another whispers back.

A hand grips his shoulder. He wants so much to fight off this person, to stand and run the last block to his workplace. Across the street he finally sees a passerby and wants to shout out to them. But the passerby either doesn't see them, or he is somehow invisible to them.

Them.

"Look at his face." The owner of the first voice comes around and faces him. Rage contorts his features. These *things* have the audacity to do this to him.

"Oh he still thinks he can get away."

"Too bad."

Before the world goes dark, Roland hears laughing at the end.

22

DESCENDANTS OF THE CURSED

Nicolette pops into view, her borrowed teleportation spell settling back into her wrist. To her left, unsurprised and waiting, is the spirit Nyxie. Past Nyxie is a group of demons, witches, spirits, and one or two werewolves, about a dozen strong. It's an odd crew, but it will work.

"What's the plan?"

Nyxie goes through and introduces them, not by name but by what they are there for. The last person she comes to is a werecoyote from Arizona. The species surprises Nicolette, not being familiar with a lot of weres besides werewolves. They are rare enough, but there are a few species out there like werecoyotes that are slowly dying out.

"We captured one of the employees responsible for the virus creation," Nyxie continues, going into some detail about their next steps. She had been largely leading this operation. Nyxie's talent for logistics surprises Nicolette, but maybe that isn't fair. She doesn't know anything about the spirit after all.

"Have you interrogated him yet?"

"Yes," she says, "but he is not giving us much information. We are hoping you can take a crack at him."

Nicolette runs her tongue over her fangs. "Vampire or witch or both?"

Nyxie grins evilly. "Yes," she says.

She looks around the room, really just a living room in a house they rented to hide in plain sight. It's a typical house in the Denver area, keeping them close to Zeusair and also keeping them invisible to their enemy. In theory at least.

The windows show a tidy front yard, two cars parked in the short driveway, and a quiet neighborhood where the kids are playing in a yard a few houses down. A werewolf in business attire carrying a couple bags of groceries comes up the drive from the trunk of the car, and heads into the front door. He shuts the front door behind him and nods at Nicolette, the newcomer.

"What happens if we can't get enough information from

him?"

"We have a backup plan," Nyxie says, glancing at the group behind her. She doesn't elaborate, and Nicolette assumes the explanation will come when she needs it. "Come down to the basement and let's give this a try."

Nicolette nods and follows her into the house's kitchen where a door leads to the basement stair. A werewolf sits casually at the kitchen table but starts when he sees the vampire come in the room. Nyxie waves him off and the wolf relaxes again. His dark eyes meet Nicolette, a mixture of curiosity and wariness in his eyes. Nicolette nods at him and gives a small smile. The werewolf raises his eyebrows and nods cordially in response.

Nicolette follows the spirit down the basement stairs cautiously. At the bottom a pair of bare lightbulbs illuminate a dim interior, all the windows covered to prevent any prying eyes. A pair of witches, another werewolf, and a demon all wait in the basement, either sitting in the rickety chairs or leaning on the walls around the room.

At the center, under one of the lightbulbs, sits a man whose appearance is both disheveled and incredibly strained. His nose at one point was bloodied, the metallic tang of which scents the air. Nicolette inhales the smell deeply, testing his bloodline from the smell. He is not a full human. He must carry genes for at least one creature line, though she couldn't quite discern which species.

Hesitating, Nicolette looks to Nyxie for permission. It is odd for her to be drinking blood without permission from the source. Her mixed heritage taught her that. Many vampires still harken from lines that once fed unabashedly from the human population. Many come from the lines that killed humans for sport. Nicolette is not from either group.

Nyxie nods, waves her forward, and steps out of her way. Nicolette approaches the man, taking a wooden chair with her to sit opposite. The man's hands are tied behind his back, keeping him firmly in the chair.

"How long has he been here?"

"Just since this morning."

Not long enough for him to be completely missed then. Nicolette silently agrees with the prudence of calling her in so early into his interrogation. She makes eye contact with the man's brown eyes, surveying his salt-and-pepper hair. Aging vampires are rare and the hair fascinates her in a morbid way.

"Do you know what I am?" she asks.

The man clears his throat and says, "Group five."

Nicolette, in confusion, looks to those around her. "They classify us into groups by species," one of the witches explains. "Vampires are group five."

"Thank you," Nicolette says politely. She turns back to the man and says, "You're not entirely right and you're not entirely wrong." She produces a single line of red light, the color a signature of her blood magic. The man's eyes widen as she takes the line of lights and wraps it around the man's neck. "This will help you tell the truth."

Fear elevates the man's heartbeat. Adrenaline colors his scent, the bitterness of fear filling her nose. She does not want to bite this man until she is ready to.

"What is your name?"

"Roland Rommel."

"What is your role with Zeusair?"

The man swallows. The tendons in his neck and face strain as he fights the spell. The red light brightens in response to his resistance. He blinks, his face twisting in anguish, and says, "I am a virologist and epidemiologist. I specialize in genetic sequencing."

"What was your role in creating the virus?"

"I designed the gene for the protein attacking your cells."

"That is as much as we've been able to get from him," the witch behind her says. "See if he will give you more."

Nicolette thinks for a moment. "Who is your leader?" she asks.

Immediately, the man clams up. The spell nearly breaks in response to his silence. It brightens then dims almost to nothing. Nicolette narrows her eyes and touches the line of light. The spell is intact but has hit a wall. There is a deeper spell or block or something in the man that is preventing him from answering. She lets out a tight breath in annoyance.

"Then we'll do this the old fashioned way," she says. With a tiny tap she releases the spell from around his neck. The man immediately tries to pull away from her and the two werewolves move to help her. She waves them off, fully capable of subduing her prey. "Don't fight," she says with the cajoling voice of a predator. "I will not cause you pain," she says.

Her left hand takes his jaw and her right clamps down on his left shoulder. She pulls him awkwardly closer to her and leans forward, smelling his neck. She first licks the curve of his neck clean of sweat, tasting his fear and anger. Then without hesitation, she sinks her fangs into his skin, taking careful aim to pierce precisely his jugular. The blood bursts from his skin. Nicolette clamps down on her prey and takes a mouthful to get a sense of the man.

Immediately, his thoughts become clear as day to her. She closes her eyes to focus better and continues to carefully sip so as not to cause him to pass out. She needs his active consciousness to understand his memories and intentions.

Please stop.

For a moment Nicolette hesitates, unused to torture and forcing a person to have their blood drank.

They'll kill me if they find out.

The thoughts betray his real concern. A woman comes to mind, thin with a scar on her hand. The woman's hard nature and steel manner fills his memory. He fears her in his bones.

They'll never find out, she whispers in his mind. *Let me understand you.*

Relief floods him, somehow giving in to her reassurance. He leans into the contact, a brief wave of guilt belying his pleasure in Nicolette's feeding. She takes a deeper draught of her prey, feeling in him the memories of his places, his background, his reason for his prejudice against their kind. All of it comes pouring out of him then, nothing held back now that he understands what she can do.

What feels like hours pass lost in the blood memories of Roland. She leans back, pulling away from his neck and licking the wound clean and closed. Her saliva closes the skin immediately, no sign of the puncture left behind.

The man looks at her, paler but otherwise healthy. His brown eyes are filled with fear and apprehension. Nicolette licks her lips, still tasting the intention behind the blood. She understands this man now.

The witch hands her a much needed glass of water. Nicolette drinks gratefully, wanting to clear the taste and sensation from her mouth. She hands the empty glass back.

"Did you get anything?"

Nicolette croaks out, "I got everything." She runs her

tongue over her fangs. "We will need a way to get into the building. Stealthily, if possible."

Nyxie nods at her words and looks at the top of the stairs calling, "Get Valence down here."

After a few moments, footsteps on the stairs signal the arrival of another person. The werecoyote comes down into the basement. His thin frame hides the strength in every move. He has blond hair and pale green eyes, his entire countenance being pale. Valence comes into the center of the room, standing next to Nicolette's chair.

"What do you think, Val?" Nyxie asks.

Valence kneels next to Roland, studying him in great detail. As Nicolette watches, his hair darkens in patches, the rest turning gray. Before long his hair is exactly the same as Roland. His features are not far behind, the dark eyes and aging skin and muscular build. Suddenly she is looking at a set of identical twins.

The real Roland turns completely pale. He looks at his twin and to Nicolette. "Is this what you meant?" he whispers to the vampire.

"I had no idea," she whispers back. "I was lying."

Alarm fills his face. He didn't consider her to be lying when he was unable to do anything but reveal the truth. A crooked smile fills Nicolette's face.

Valence stands up and steps away from the pair. Nicolette

stretches and follows Valence up the stairs. "Make sure he has something with iron and calcium in it," she says. "Some broth or some juice would help."

As Valence walks through the threshold into the kitchen, the werewolf at the table starts at the sight of him but calms immediately when the rest come through behind him. "Valence?" he says.

"Yeah," the shifter answers. "Sorry I didn't warn you."

The werewolf snorts. "You never do." Nicolette's confusion must show because the werewolf adds, "Valence and I go way back. We're both from Arizona."

Nyxie hands Nicolette a bottle of water and a cinnamon roll, both of which tempt her churning stomach. She takes a seat at the table with the werewolf, Valence joining them and accepting a cinnamon roll eagerly.

To Nyxie she says, "Can I have a glass please?" The spirit doesn't question it. To Valence she asks, "You're a werecoyote but also a shapeshifter? I thought shifters were extinct."

Valence raises and lowers a shoulder. "I'm not actually a shifter," he says. "My mother's side can be traced back to the last surviving shifters almost a thousand years ago. The last few we know of anyway," he says. "They were hermits in upper Canada."

The hermetic lifestyle would have kept them isolated from what they now know was a plague that wiped them out. The hermit lifestyle triggers something in Nicolette's memory from her childhood. "The Cursed," she says.

Valence's slight smile on Roland's borrowed face chills her. "Yes," he says. "We are sometimes called that by vampires and demons both."

An amused look comes over her face. "Descendants of the Cursed," she muses. "I never knew they were shapeshifters. Legends said your people were specters or ghosts, with forms that could not be seen." She takes a bite of her forgotten cinnamon roll. Nyxie hands her the glass she requested.

"What's that for?" the werewolf asks.

"Sorry, what's your name?" Nicolette asks, realizing she doesn't know.

The werewolf smiles and says, "Kenyon."

"Kenyon," she repeats. "I asked for the glass because I didn't think Valence would enjoy drinking my blood from my wrist or neck."

The look of shock on both of their faces almost makes her laugh. Clearly they hadn't expected that response.

She explains, "If you want to pass for Roland, you need to have his memories and mannerisms. If you drink my blood, you can gain that."

Shocked silence fills the room. The witch who had followed them up looks at Nicolette in a clinical way. "Is that partially witchcraft?" she inquires.

Nicolette smiles at the woman with graying black hair and nods. "I've found it works well enough to emulate the power of a vampire."

The witch shakes her head in surprise. "Blood magic and vampirism. No wonder the Royal Court likes having you around."

A blush fills Nicolette's cheeks for a moment. She is embarrassed by the compliment. By way of answer, she extracts a tiny knife from her belt and looks at Valence. "Are you ready for this?"

"Would it work better from your wrist?" he asks.

"Yes," she concedes.

"I'm not squeamish. I can handle it from your wrist," he says.

"If you insist."

Carefully she slices into her wrist, a line of red flaring up where the blade traces. She scooches her chair closer to Valence and offers the wrist before so much as a drop of blood has fallen to the table. Valence delicately lifts her wrist to his mouth and, after a pause and some consideration, he latches on. Immediately Nicolette feels the pull of the blood and carefully filters it to give him what he needs.

"I have to say I'm impressed," Kenyon says.

Nyxie and the witch both nod in agreement.

A few minutes later Nicolette cradles Valence's chin up and

away from her wrist. She licks her wrist, her saliva serving to heal the open wound almost immediately. Nyxie thinks to give a paper towel to the shifter and he wipes his mouth, licking his lips before doing so. No blood marks the paper towel. Nicolette is impressed with the tidy way he drank her blood. She stows the knife back into her belt.

"Do you have what you need?"

Valence seems to be thinking, his face vague with deep thought. "I think so," he says. He nods slowly, mulling something over. "I think we should proceed. The security is heavy, but I can get through."

Nyxie straightens up. "I'll get the team ready. We'll have you go tomorrow."

Nicolette takes another bite of the cinnamon roll, feeling the sustenance would be necessary.

23

INTELLIGENT ROBOTS

Oriphine pipettes a viscous sample of DNA into several holes in a gel electrophoresis sheet. She is precise in the extreme, using her refined spirit muscles to do the work that requires dexterity. Finished, she places the remaining DNA into its sample tube and dumps the pipette tip into a biohazard disposal bin. She lets out a breath and leans back from the lab hood, her gloved hands still on the other side of the vent. Carefully, she removes those gloves, tosses them into a biohazard trash bin, and pulls her hands out, shutting the hood. She goes to wash her hands.

"All set?" Greg asks.

Oriphine nods. This is their sixteenth sample thus far. She took over for Kai so her lovely witch could take the time to breathe and grieve. It had been about seventy years since she had worked in a medical lab, but the memories still feel fresh. So she got into the swing of it relatively easily with Greg's guidance.

"Thank you for helping," Greg says. He has gotten comfortable with having so many creatures around him, and indeed the rest of the lab staff has as well, but sometimes his surprise and awe shows that the situation really is unusual.

"I appreciate your help," she answers. "It's been quite a while since I've done this kind of work."

"When did you work in a lab?" Greg's curiosity is one of his endearing qualities.

"I worked in a medical lab in a MASH unit back in the 50s. Not the same thing, but it's helpful experience," she says.

"Were you a doctor? Or a nurse?"

"A nurse," she says. "I blended in more easily that way. And I had prior experience from the great wars."

Greg looks surprised. "Forgive me, but how did you pass for human?"

With a wide smile, Oriphine answers, "In war times few people pay attention to the details. I was just another nurse with her hair in a bun and a mask covering her face."

Greg's eyes go to her mask and back up to her hair. At the moment her hair is a dark black, almost dark as the night sky, and her eyes match a deep brown. "And the uniform helped," he says.

"Yes, but I also looked like those around me back then. I pick up the other's traits sometimes, and that was one of those times."

The door opens and one of Greg's colleagues steps through. "Are you ready for me?" she asks.

"Yeah, we're ready," Greg answers.

Somehow the humans Greg works with have gotten used to the influx of creatures and barely react to them all now. Oriphine occasionally suspects witchcraft at work, but she would smell the magic. No, it's just that they've all been around enough that they've almost become normal to see. Even someone like her whose appearance is noticeably inhuman.

"I think we should take a break," Greg says. He removes his gloves and deposits them in a biohazard bin and washes his hands. He leads Oriphine out of the lab. On the other side of the door, he says, "Coffee?"

Reading his intentions, she can see he is still curious about her and wants to know more about her. "I could drink some coffee," she says. He is relieved that she said yes. As they walk she asks, "Do you need many hands to help with the lab work?"

He shrugs. "Until they invent intelligent robots to do it for us, then yes," he answers. "I usually have some interns running around, but I moved them all to a less hazardous lab for the time being. No need to expose them."

Oriphine nods. She wonders how the world would have been if the same approaches had been put in place during the great plagues of the past. How different the history of humanity could have been.

Once they are in the breakroom and have gotten their coffee, they take a table together. Oriphine checks her phone and sees a message from Kai telling her she is ok but working through her grief. She tells Oriphine she'll be into the lab later in the afternoon. Oriphine puts her phone away and takes a sip of the CDC's breakroom coffee. As coffee goes it could be much worse. She takes a deeper drink and lets the warmness soothe her. Though she has lived a long time and has the experience to match, their current situation still gives her anxiety.

"May I ask a personal question?" Greg says suddenly.

"Of course."

"How old are you?"

Oriphine laughs. Humans never stop being obsessed with her age. When in reality her answer is the truth. "I've lost track," she says. "I was born in an ancient time and I've seen a lot since then."

"How do you keep up with it all?" he asks.

Oriphine raises and lowers a shoulder and takes another sip of her okay coffee. "I don't try to, really," she says. "I remember things, a lot of them really. But not actively. It all comes back to me as needed and sometimes unsummoned."

Greg is staring at her in deep contemplation. It's almost as if he's looking past Oriphine instead of at her. "Is it hard to relate to younger people?"

She smiles at him, understanding why he is asking her. The connection between him and the vampire prince is undeniable and really obvious to anyone with eyes. No doubt he wonders if they would ever be on even footing.

"Yes and no," she answers. "I wouldn't look to Kai to understand what it was like during the fall of the Roman Empire, for example. But we connect on the fundamentals. On what it's like to be a creature or just a person trying to find their way in the world. That's what really matters."

Greg looks at her as if he really sees her now. "I understand," he says. "Thank you."

Oriphine doesn't answer. She continues to sip her coffee as she replies to Kai. So much joy a few words between them gives her.

24

NOISES BEHIND THE DOOR

Lovell woke to his alarm early in the pre-dawn hours. Lincoln groans and rolls over, barely disturbed by the sound of the clock going off. Lovell envies him for his sleep. He's on duty in twenty minutes in the hospital ward and likes to get down there early. He gets up and gets dressed in some comfortable joggers and a workout tee. The morning air might be too chilly for it, but the hazmat suits are uncomfortably hot if worn for more than ten minutes. He learned the hard way to wear comfortable clothes.

Five minutes and a quick protein shake later he is down in

the tent outside the guest house donning a hazmat suit. Lovell feels resigned to the day ahead of him, standing guard in thirty-minute shifts over the Alpha and Luna. Part of him feels like it's only a matter of time before the virus takes them. Still he does his duty and continues to stand watch.

Lovell itches his nose before closing the headpiece. He finds the whole thing uncomfortable, but the worst part is his nose always itches once he's in the suit. Once satisfied and completely suited up, he heads for his shift in the house.

As usual, the guest house is quiet. It's been that way for a while now. Too many of their people are dying and the ones that are merely severely ill seem to be holding their collective breaths waiting for death to come. Not enough of them are surviving.

Lovell starts his rounds by going into the downstairs ward, the room that once hosted parties and other pack functions. The oversize ballroom/meeting room had been cleared of the large dining table and all chairs. Cots had been brought in as beds for the less ill among them. If a patient spent their entire time in this ward, they were doing better than most.

For some reason their percentages are skewed compared to the rest of the population. The group at the CDC suspected the variant attacking the pack is particularly virulent and deadly. About half of those in this ward would wind up in an upstairs ventilator ward. About half of those would not leave the house alive. The grim numbers weighed on every person providing medical care. Lincoln expressed worry on a regular basis about Lovell's duties in the house. But there is nothing that could be done. They all needed to pitch in and provide as much help as they could.

Lovell finishes checking the security in the lower ward. This is never the ward he worries about. The Alpha and Luna are upstairs in the critical ward. Once Esyn died they seemed to give up. They are two of the strongest people he knows, but even they couldn't hold up against the grief of losing a child.

Lovell makes his way up the stairs and to the first ward on the left. The less critical patients on ventilators are here. Some of these ventilators were improvised or shared between patients. They figured out how to split the ventilator feed, how to MacGuyver a basic ventilator with spare parts or old anesthesia machines, and anything they could to make do with what they had. Sometimes it worked. Sometimes it didn't.

The lone nurse on duty greets Lovell as he passes through, checking windows and the side doors to make sure they are secure. This side of the building was also a dorm for visiting packs. At one point thirty pack warriors from the Crescent Pack, visiting from Louisiana, slept in this ward. Now it housed everyone from young children to elderly pack members. The sight caused a sinking feeling in his gut.

He moved on.

The last ward he always checks is where the Alpha and Luna are being treated. Both had been put in induced comas since they fell gravely ill right after their daughter's death. He approaches the ward and hears odd noises behind the door.

For a moment he pauses, his heckles going up in reaction to a perceived danger. What danger could there be here? Cautiously he opens the door and steps through. The only person he sees right away is a sleeping nurse. She is slumped over in a chair at the side of the door.

Immediately Lovell checks on her. She seems to be deeply asleep and barely breathing. He is not a medical professional but even he can see that she is in danger. Then he realizes who the other person is in the room. Josiah Fredegund stands by the Alpha's bed injecting something into his IV. For some reason the sight sends a shiver down Lovell's spine. Something isn't right here.

Josiah sees Lovell and greets him genially. His eyes go to the nurse and he says, "She collapsed a few minutes ago. I'm going to take her down to the downstairs ward. I'm afraid she's fallen ill."

This seems strange to Lovell as he had just seen this nurse yesterday fully healthy and in no way ill enough to be in the ward downstairs.

Josiah continues, "Could you help me get her downstairs?" He caps the syringe in his hand and begins walking toward

Lovell.

Even more so Lovell's instincts are telling him he is in danger. But what kind of danger could he be from the pack doctor? And could he just run and leave the nurse here?

As Josiah closes in, he makes up his mind. His gloved hand on the door behind him, he turns the knob and makes to move through.

Josiah raises a hand and says something in a language he doesn't know.

Whatever power Josiah called hits Lovell in the chest and he begins to slump to the ground. It is not enough to take him out completely. He lunges at Josiah, the only power he has being brute strength.

Josiah reacts like a well-trained pack warrior and dodges the lunge. He uncaps the syringe in his hand. In one swift motion he stabs Lovell through the material of his hazmat suit. Lovell absently wonders how as the suit is relatively indelible. Josiah must have used some power to do it.

Power.

Josiah is part witch? How did no one know this?

The good doctor hits him with power again, this time bringing Lovell all the way to the ground. And then hits him again and again until Lovell can feel consciousness beginning to slip away.

"I can't kill you yet," the doctor whispers. "But be assured

I'll rid the world of you and your kind."

"You're one of us," Lovell gasps out, his heart shuddering unevenly.

"I am an abomination like you. And don't worry. I'll take care of myself when the time comes," he says.

How deranged Josiah must be to feel that way. Lincoln was right to worry.

Lincoln.

Fear fills him at the thought that his partner might be in danger too.

Then the darkness takes him and he can't think about anything anymore.

25

INSTINCTS TAKING OVER

Nicolette stands in the kitchen, one of the dozen people huddled around the table where Valence sits giving his report. Anger courses through her as she listens to what he found out about the missing vampire. Anger she could control but is unwilling to try to control. The only thing she wants right now is vengeance.

The general feeling around the room is the same.

"Did you get a chance to examine the vampire?" Nicolette asks.

"No," Valence answers. "She was behind a glass barrier.

She looked at me and I think she could tell I wasn't the other Roland, but she kept it to herself."

"Good," Nyxie says. "The last thing we need is a blown cover." She pauses and considers for a moment. "I think when we do this, we need to do this all at once. Not just a rescue mission and not just a mission to destroy their research. We do it all or we do nothing. And nothing is not an option."

"When should we go?"

"Late," Valence says. "There is a guard shift change at eleven tonight. We can slip in then and get to the labs without being detected. There are guards overnight but they don't talk to each other except in extreme cases."

Murmurs run through the room as the gathered werewolves, witches, hybrids, and everyone else talk about the coming raid. Nicolette knows she will be on that team, her combination of magic and vampire power being too useful to not be on it. She is the only vampire in the room. All she knows is she's getting her sister vampire out one way or another.

"I think we can teleport in and out if I initiate it," Nyxie says, her voice cutting through the others. "Do they have magic sensors?"

"They do," Valence says. "But I'm not sure they would pick up on spirit magic as they don't have enough on spirits to even develop the virus."

Nyxie nods and then stands from the kitchen table. "Be prepared to go tonight, ready to leave by ten forty-five and no later. We'll meet in the living room and I'll teleport everyone at once."

The various creatures around the room indicate their understanding. Nicolette thinks to herself that she should feed before she has to go on this mission in four hours. The clock on the wall reads 6:17. She has time to go eat properly. As the room clears out, she heads in the direction Nyxie goes. The spirit sees her coming and stops to talk to her.

"Can you teleport me somewhere I can feed?"

Nyxie seems surprised. "I can, but why not feed on one of us."

Nicolette is taken aback by the idea. "Most creatures would not appreciate it, nor would I want to weaken anyone just prior to a high risk trip like this."

Nyxie seems to consider it for a moment. "Well, why not take my blood? Corporealness is incidental to spirits. We don't need our blood as much as other species do."

The idea blows through Nicolette. She is stunned she never thought of feeding on a spirit or that she never considered a spirit wouldn't need blood as much as the others. Curiosity is getting the better of her. Her hunter instincts begin to focus on Nyxie.

"Would you really be ok with it?" she asks softly.

"Yes, I would."

Nicolette glances around, seeing no one has been privy to their conversation, and whispers back, "We should go somewhere private."

"Upstairs."

Nicolette stops Nyxie as she turns to head for the staircase. "I'm warning you," she says softly. "You might not like what I learn about you from this."

Nyxie squeezes her hand and says, "I'm not worried. After the thousand plus years I've seen, you will only get a small slice of me."

Nicolette nods and together they walk up the stairs to find a quiet bedroom. Nyxie shuts the door and waits expectantly for direction. Nicolette takes a seat on the bed and gestures for Nyxie to join her. She places a hand on Nyxie's shoulder, her instincts taking over now. The smell of Nyxie skin is almost overpowering, the scent of spirits being so much stronger than humans or any other species. Nicolette leans into Nyxie's neckline and gently inhales, finding the best place to bite down. She senses Nyxie's nervousness, a fact that only spurs her instincts on rather than pulling her back.

Gently, Nicolette cradles Nyxie's head and leans her nose into the spirit's neck. In another second her fangs make contact and the warm, rich blood of a thousand plus year old spirit spills into Nicolette's mouth.

Some twenty minutes pass. Nicolette doesn't pay attention to the time. She only carefully and slowly pulls the blood from Nyxie with a delicacy akin to unspooling thread. When a sufficient amount of the spirit's thick blood has crossed her lips, she gently stops the flow and licks the wound clean. Her saliva would close the puncture marks in a moment and there would be no indication that she drank from Nyxie.

The spirit settles into Nicolette's arms and rests, gathering her strength Nicolette presumes. Losing blood for any species is a big deal, though as Nyxie said it might not be as critical for a spirit. In either case she doesn't mind waiting while Nyxie recoups herself. They would all need to be at full strength to get through tonight.

Finally, after enough time has passed, they leave the bedroom and head downstairs. In the kitchen and the living room, they find their forces beginning to gather. Valence still looks like Roland just in case they run into anyone. As for the rest, it feels like the room is armed to the teeth, ready to get into a skirmish. And really most of them are werewolves so they are literally armed with teeth.

Nicolette absently runs her tongue over her fangs and thinks casually about killing whoever kidnapped their missing vampire. But in a moment she has focused and let go of the anger within. This mission needs to be precise even if it would end in explosions and flames.

As the clock draws closer to 10:45, the room begins to fill. Nyxie checks each team around the room. Each group signals their readiness. With everyone in place, they are ready to begin.

"Link up," Nyxie says.

One by one, creature after creature takes a hand of the one next to them. Nyxie takes Nicolette's hand, and Nicolette links with Valence and so on and so on. As soon as everyone has linked up together, Nyxie looks around the room and nods.

"Let's go," Nyxie says.

Nicolette's sight goes dark as Nyxie teleports them out.

26

DEATH OF AN ALPHA

So much death in the past few weeks. So much darkness. It was enough to turn even the kindest souls to evil.

Chloe stands at the side of the pack, not wanting to be near the center of attention though some think she has the right to be. She has fought so hard for every pack member to survive the plague. But they could not all survive. In fact, more and more of them are dying. She looks across the crowd to Josiah and wonders how frustrated he must be in the face of so much death. Here they stand, watching the body of the latest dead and they must carry on.

As one, the family of the Beta turns to the moon and begins to shed their clothes. The rest of the pack follows suit. They would go on one final run through the woods together to honor the fallen. Chloe feels the changes coming over her body, the power in the muscles and the sprouting of fur. Before long she is standing with her chestnut fur, a luxurious coat enveloping her. She is not as large as other wolves which is to be expected given her age. But she is strong and she can feel that strength holding her up in the face of her grief.

Together.

The Beta calls them out and the pack begins to run towards the tree line. Chloe falls to the back of the pack pausing as she passes the bodies of the dead on their dais. As the pack leaves, the bodies will be burned. Even through the wrappings on their bodies she can still smell the strong scent of the pair.

She thought Esyn's death would be the worst she had to face. But here, standing and staring at their bodies in wolf form, she feels a pain from grief she cannot comprehend. It infects her very bones with anguish and taints her optimism with darkness. She takes a deep breath to inhale the pair's scents one last time. Then she follows the receding pack into the woods and gives herself away to instinct.

Still she cannot shake either the image or the scent of the fallen. So many they've had to burn in the past weeks. So many have died and so many more are gravely ill. Too many friends have fallen for her to feel immune. She thought she would go numb to the pain. She thought she had gone numb. But she hadn't. And she isn't. The pain follows her into the trees, into the night, into the darkness of the forest.

Behind her she can scent the first tendrils of smoke and knows if she looks back she would see the plume going into the sky. The last of their line, the bodies burn to wipe away the possibility of infection. Every single body burned saves lives.

Next to her Josiah comes up and nudges her in comfort. He knows the pain she feels and she lowers her head for a moment in deference to that pain. Then she turns and puts her speed into her stride to carry on fighting. She fights the anguish and the pain and the heavy feeling of grief settling in her body so that she can run this final run for the dead.

At the top of the ridge ahead of her, the howls begin to lift into the night. She joins their ranks and lifts her own mournful voice to the cacophony. The night echoes with wolf grief.

If she could cry in this form she would. Instead she shows her grief with her howling voice and the lowering of her tail. Somewhere below them the plume of smoke continues to rise. Somewhere below them the bodies burn.

Chloe silently says her final goodbyes to their Alpha and Luna.

Josiah joins her, not howling but looking subdued. She looks over at him and the two meet eyes. A wave of anxious realization comes over her. With so much death in their pack, if they couldn't find the answer, what would become of their pack? Already their numbers dwindle and they cannot find a way to stop the infections from spreading. Nothing they do stops the spread. Nothing.

Then it hits her.

Even kind hearts can turn evil.

Could the infections be coming from someone inside the pack? Could there be someone deliberately infecting their pack members?

She looks around at the remaining pack, some forty wolves all howling to the moon in pain. So many pack warriors had died. The pack weakens daily.

One of us, she thinks. It had to be a traitor.

But who could betray their own kind? Who *would?*

And worse, who could be vile enough to kill children?

She has no answers. And that frightens her worse than the death of an Alpha.

27

MOTIONLESS ON THE FLOOR

Nicolette's sight clears as they pop into existence within the Zeusair building.

Her initial disorientation passes and she takes in her surroundings. It is as Val described it. They find themselves in a long hallway with glass walls on either side. On the other side of the glass walls she can make out laboratories and office spaces. She couldn't imagine working in such a fishbowl.

The group starts moving around after a pause to see if any alarms will go off. Val, still looking like Roland, moves toward one office in particular. Nicolette sees the nameplate and realizes the office is Roland's. Val lets them into the office and one of the more tech savvy wolves sits down and begins pulling all the records off the system. The rest fan out and head into other labs and down the hall to destroy samples and computers and everything else they can. They are stealing the records for sure, but they are also not going to leave anything behind.

"Where's the vampire?" Nicolette asks Val.

"Ninth floor. I'll take you."

Kenyon breaks away from the group and says, "I'll come with you."

A couple others go with them, but Nyxie notably stays on that floor ready to get everyone out if necessary. "Don't stay too long," she warns. They all know at any point they could trigger a silent alarm and need to leave immediately.

Val takes them to the elevator bank. The six of them pile in, Nicolette uncomfortably close to Kenyon. After a few tense minutes, they step out onto the ninth floor. They find the place deserted. One of the wolves steps behind the security desk.

"There's a feed from the cameras here. I'm going to see if I can switch to the exterior feed so we can get a head's up in case we trip an alarm." He lofts a walkie talkie and adds, "I'll radio if there's trouble."

Nicolette nods but she is focused on the task at hand. One

of her sisters is somewhere on this floor. She follows Val closely with Kenyon and the other two following close behind.

Several turns take them to a dimly lit hallway with ubiquitous doors on either side. Val takes them to a door marked "7526" and indicates to the wolves to open it. One of them removes the door from its hinges. Again they find the place deserted.

There a thick glass wall separates them from the cell. Only a dim light built into the cell ceiling illuminates the gray cell interior. In that gray interior they find the vampire.

There she lay, motionless on the floor.

Something snaps inside Nicolette. Though the pane of glass separating her from the fallen sister must be several inches thick, she balls up a fist and slams her knuckles into it. Behind the hit is every ounce of magic and vampiric strength she has.

The glass shatters.

"Remind me not to piss you off," Val mutters, his voice subdued with awe.

Nicolette ignores him. She steps through the broken glass, hearing the satisfying crunch beneath her boots. The vampire is completely unconscious and barely breathing. There are burns on her wrists and ankles from the prolonged exposure to mercury there. The shackles on her look incredibly painful. Nicolette is only slightly allergic to mercury, but she still does her best to avoid it. Rather than reach out and take them off, she uses her magic. With a simple spell she unlocks the shackles and they fall open. Delicately she uses the tips of two fingers to pull the chains away from the vampire's arms and legs. She feels a pang of guilt as they scrape her leg and leave a pale burn mark there.

Gradually the vampire wakes up. At first she opens her eyes groggily, but then her vision clamps on Nicolette who is undeniably vampiric. Suddenly she is alert and looking around, rubbing her wrists where they were burned.

"What's your name?" Nicolette asks. Even the American Vampire Regime did not give her name.

"Erylis," she says quietly.

"I'm Nicolette. I work for the Royal Court," she says. "Can you stand?"

"I can try."

Nicolette offers her hand and Erylis takes it. She is too weak to get up on her own and when she is standing Nicolette takes most of her weight. Kenyon comes up and goes to Erylis's other side. The vampire looks quizzically at the large werewolf but does not protest when he slings her arm around his neck.

"May I carry you?" he asks.

Erylis agrees. Kenyon lifts her like she weighs nothing and slings her legs over his other arm.

"We gotta go," Val says suddenly. "The silent alarm went off. We have to get back to the sixth floor."

Without hesitation and with a general sense of panic, they head out of the cell. In the hallway they find the other two werewolves with about five other captives freed from cells. None of them look too good. Three werewolves and a pair of witches stare at them with a mixture of fear and relief.

"Let's go," she says hurriedly.

They follow Val back up the hallways to the security desk. They find the werewolf there looking up at them in relief. On the screen she can see the mass of cars that have rolled up to the Zeusair building. The security officers on the first floor also look panicked.

The lights go out.

After a moment while the emergency lighting comes in, Kenyon says, "We should take the stairs.

The head for the stairwell around the corner from the elevator. Val pulls on the door handle. For the first time all night Nicolette fears they won't make it out of the building.

The door to the stairwell is sealed shut.

28

SOMETHING NEFARIOUS

"The numbers don't make sense," Greg says.

Adin is inclined to agree though he doesn't really understand all the details of immunology. The hour is very late but none of them sleep much anymore. Instead they are all sitting around a table in one of the CDC conference rooms discussing the latest pandemic numbers. Greg had called the late night meeting because he was concerned the numbers weren't making sense.

Adin looks around the table at Kai, Oriphine, Ezra, and Lairlux next to him. "Let's go through it one more time?" he says, unsure if he is the only one that needs the explanation.

Kai speaks up and says, "Yes, one more time. To be sure."

Greg spreads several pages of graphs out on the table. "These are the numbers for all the clusters we have here in the US and a couple in nearby countries. We aren't tracking everyone which is what made me think it was an anomaly." He pulls three more charts from his folder and lays them out. "These three clusters are still growing. Every other cluster saw a plateau with the start of mitigation measures, the masks and isolation et cetera." He points to the graphs and pulls one of the others to compare it to. "Look at the increase."

They all lean over the table and check the numbers against each other. There is a notable increase. The numbers are trending upward at an alarming rate, a rate not seen since the first week of the pandemic.

"Look, I'm not saying something nefarious is happening," Greg says. "I'm just saying these clusters look more virulent but for no reason. The strains are the same as others but it's like they are more contagious somehow."

"Maybe we need to resequence them," Kai suggests.

"I have samples coming," Greg says. "But I'm not sure how much it'll help explain this."

"Hm, I agree," Oriphine says. "But it can't hurt to check it out. What are the other options?"

There is a pause as Greg considers his next words carefully.

"If it's not a more contagious variant, then our other options are a secondary virus infecting all three clusters," he says with a dubious tone. "Or," and here he pauses again, "we have a mole."

There is silence that greets his words. Then Oriphine says, "You mean someone is deliberately infecting the clusters."

Greg nods slowly. He looks at Ezra with a grim expression. Vampires are naturally suspicious of people, but this time Adin is inclined to agree. The possibility is sitting right in front of them, the evidence on the pages and pages of graphs.

"There's a slim possibility it's a secondary infection, but I don't know how three isolated clusters could all have gotten the same thing," Oriphine says. She looks at Kai with concern in her ancient spirit eyes. "And the likelihood of it being multiple infections is even lower."

"Yes, that's what I think," Greg says.

Ezra, who remained silent until now, says, "I'm inclined to believe it is something nefarious, though even I must admit it is difficult to believe one of our own kind would betray us. Much less three minimum."

"Where are the clusters?"

Greg lifts the pages. "The San Francisco witch's coven, the Manitoba pack, and the Swifttooth pack."

Kai flinches visibly. "Has anyone talked to Chloe?"

Greg purses his lips before saying, "She agrees with us.

Their Alpha just died. It occurred to her that the cases kept rising and their numbers were dwindling too quickly for it to be normal."

"I think she might be right."

"Does she have any idea who the mole could be?" Oriphine asks.

"No," Greg says.

"What about the Zeusair team? Any word from them?"

"They've gone radio silent as of an hour ago," Ezra says. "Nicolette said they are going into the lab. We should have the Zeusair data tonight."

Kai shakes her head in disbelief. "This just feels so wrong," she says. "Just knowing how many people have died and how many creatures are infected."

"I know," Greg says. "I just can't ignore the data."

They lapse into silence, Oriphine hunched over reading the graphs and the rest just exchanging grim looks.

"Then we should wait for the Zeusair data," Lairlux says. "I think that would be best."

"I agree."

Greg's phone goes off. He checks it and inhales quickly. "They're in. They just sent us a zip file."

Immediately everyone else begins checking their phones.

"I got it too." Kai's brow furrows. "I'm going to go start pulling the data onto my laptop."

"Me too," Ezra says.

"Let's meet back in the morning when we've had a chance to look it over."

"I'm probably staying here tonight," Kai admits. "I don't think I'll be able to sleep after this."

Adin glances at Lairlux and she nods her head every so slightly. "I think we're staying too," he says.

"Alright, let's give them an hour then," Greg says. He is still enthralled with the emails on his phone. "Meet back here then?" He looks around the group.

"One hour."

The group breaks up and they leave the conference room. Adin takes Lairlux's hand. She squeezes it. Somehow things feel so much worse than they did only an hour ago.

29

BURN IT TO THE GROUND

"We have to go," Nyxie says.

Several voices agree with her.

"What about the other group?"

"They're trapped on the ninth floor," the techie werewolf working at Roland's computer says. "I can see them outside the stairwell."

"Show me," Nyxie says. She rounds the desk in Roland's office and peers at the screen. She takes in the details and the location. "Okay I can go get them. But we should get everyone out of this floor first."

"What should we do about the labs?"

There is silence that meets his words. Then one voice says, "Burn it to the ground."

And no one argues.

"Can you disable the fire suppression system?" she asks.

"I can try." The techie wolf goes back to the computer and presumably begins to work on disabling the fire suppression system.

"Will that unseal the doors?" she asks.

"No," he says. "That looks like it's part of a security system. We tripped something by going into one of the labs."

"Probably the DNA lab," a voice grumbles.

Nyxie is inclined to agree.

"Done."

"You heard the man. Burn it all."

To Nyxie the techie wolf says, "You should go get them now. It'll take a minute to get everything ready to burn."

She nods and agrees. She concentrates on the image from the screen. Internally she pulls herself inward and blinks out of the sixth floor.

A fraction of a second later she is standing on the landing of the ninth floor looking at a larger-than-expected group of wolves, witches, and vampires. She is met with wide eyes from several of them. And looking at their numbers, the ones she doesn't recognize look like they are in rough shape.

"Nyxie!" Nicolette says. "Can you get us out of here?"

"Let me take you to the sixth floor. I'll take everyone back from there. We're getting ready to burn."

"Link up."

The group scrambles to hold each other's hands or shoulders or whatever body part is closest to them. They form an odd spider's web with Nyxie grabbing the wolf closest to her. She reaches through the contact to all the creatures touching, right down to Kenyon whose elbow is being held by Nicolette. She pulls inward and yanks the whole group with her.

They appear on the sixth floor, the smell of fire accelerant immediately filling her nose.

"We're ready."

A low explosion comes from the direction of the elevator bank. The floor reverberates beneath them. One of the panes of glass shatters. She thought it was bulletproof but maybe it couldn't stand up to an explosion.

"Change of plans. Take as many as you can now. I'll get the rest together."

"Not me," Nicolette says, stepping away from Kenyon. She grabs the hand of a witch standing near to her and puts it on Kenyon's elbow. "I can defend our people while you get them out."

Nyxie nods without words. She reaches out again to the

group and yanks them through to the house. The living room suddenly feels cramped. "Go into the kitchen," she says. "I need this room to teleport."

She doesn't wait for a reply or for them to start moving. She just pulls inward and jumps back to the lab. She appears in the middle of a firefight.

Fortunately she has dealt with conflicts before. She lifts her right forearm in the direction of the oncoming forces. An energy shield appears in a low glowing gold. Bullets fly in her direction. She realizes she is an ample target for them to hit.

A bullet hits her shield and disintegrates in mid air.

To her right there is a werewolf on the floor, the blood pooling around him telling her he doesn't have much time. If he has any time left. Behind her several wolves run into a lab. She finally spots Nicolette between her and the oncoming humans.

She watches in horror and awe as the human closest to her drops to the ground, the blood oozing out of him through his skin. Nyxie's stomach turns. She had never seen anything like it.

Bullets fly in Nicolette's direction. One hits home on her right shoulder. Nicolette immediately retaliates. She flattens two of the humans near her. Even though the human is wearing full swat gear, she can make out the broken bones and the blood coming out of him.

"Nicolette!" Nyxie calls. The vampire glances back and begins retreating to where she stands.

"Get them out of here."

Nyxie nods. She goes into the lab where the remaining wolves hover. Two more of them have been wounded, either by the glass or from bullets. She signals to them to link up.

"We need to set the fire," one of them says.

"Leave it to me."

She takes their hands. The glass shatters behind her. She pulls inward and yanks them back to the house. Again the living room feels crowded.

"Get them into the kitchen or one of the bedrooms."

She doesn't wait. She immediately teleports back to the sixth floor of Zeusair. She raises the shield. With her free hand she sets the fire in the lab. Smoke beings to fill her nose.

Nicolette has backed up to where the fallen wolf lays. He isn't moving. Nyxie runs up to them. Nicolette's shoulder is bleeding badly and she has taken another hit to her leg. Her magic lags as she throws everything she has at the oncoming humans.

Nyxie grabs the ankle of the wolf. She reaches out and grabs Nicolette's injured leg. Nicolette winces and lowers her hands. In one swift move Nyxie drops the shield and yanks them back to the house.

Nicolette collapses on the nearest couch.

"We need a healer." The voice comes from the kitchen. Kenyon comes into the kitchen. "We lost one of them. We need a healer before we lose any more." His eyes fall to Nicolette on the couch.

Nyxie pulls out her phone and texts the group. She is afraid that even with teleportation they won't get here fast enough.

Nicolette passes out. She is losing too much blood, even for a vampire.

She checks the wolf on the floor. She finds no pulse.

Kenyon checks on Nicolette. "She's fading. We need a vampire."

Three people appear. She recognizes the vampire prince though she does not know him. The other two, Oriphine and Kai, head for the kitchen.

The vampire prince slices his wrist open with a small knife and tips Nicolette's head back. He opens her mouth and lets his blood flow into her. For a moment Nyxie is transfixed by the sight. Then she shakes herself and follows the other two into the kitchen. Kenyon stays behind to help with Nicolette. She admires his iron stomach.

On the kitchen table one wolf and one of the witches lay side by side. Absently Nyxie wonders who makes a table that can hold the weight. She sets the thought aside and briefly watches as Oriphine works on the wolf and Kai works on the witch. The witch had been one of the captives and looked worse than any of the others. No doubt she was one of the first taken.

"Nyxie."

She turns to find the techie wolf whose name she finally remembers is Kit. He is standing at the kitchen counter with a laptop in front of him. She goes to stand next to him and looks over his shoulder.

Kit pulls up a chart from one of the Zeusair files. She glances over it but doesn't see what he sees.

"We have a problem," Kit whispers. "This set of data is from the Swifttooth pack."

"What do you mean?"

"This data is only two weeks old. And some of these samples are from only two days ago."

It takes a moment. Then it clicks.

"Someone is feeding them information."

Kai comes to the kitchen sink and washes her hands. "What's going on?"

Kit looks up with a grim expression on his face. "There's a mole in the Swifttooth pack." Kit points a set of letters on the dataset. "Know anyone with those initials? Anyone at Swifttooth?"

The witch's expression suddenly goes very dark. "I do." With a clenched jaw she adds, "And I think I know who killed Asa."

Nyxie's eyebrows go up. "Who?"

Kai tells her.

30

INTO THE NIGHT

Chloe waits silently next to the guest house, her entire body in shadow. She needs to wait till the guards change before she goes inside. She unlocked the back door earlier in the day when she was in there in full hazmat gear. She knows she's taking a chance going in without gear, but she needs to know. She pulls the N95 mask from her pocket and puts it on.

Her watch reads three in the morning. Chloe's wolf ears listen for the sound of the front door creaking. She hears it and makes her way to the back door. She delicately turns the handle, careful not to make a sound. A minute later she is creeping through the dark interior up the stairs to the main ward.

There just to the left of the doorway is a cabinet that doesn't fully close. Chloe is not a large wolf and she eyeballed the interior earlier in the week. She determined that she could fit in the cabinet well enough to be hidden. Quietly and carefully so as not to disturb a patient, she opens the cabinet and climbs inside. She closes the door all the way it will go which is to say there is a crack between the doors. She pulls her phone out of her pocket, turns off the ringer, all her alarms, and the flash for the camera. Then she waits.

About an hour passes. The silence and the cramped space bother Chloe, but she refuses to give up. She believes she knows who is responsible. She just needs to prove it.

The door to the ward opens and closes. Her vantage point doesn't give her much of a view beyond what is directly in front of her. Still she starts recording on her phone while she waits.

It takes a few minutes before the person in the hazmat suit comes into view. They approach one of the patient tables, appear to be checking vitals, and then they stop and pull out a vial from the pocket of their suit. The person draws up an amount of the liquid within, taps the needle, and then injects it into the IV fluid bag. The patient she recognizes as Lovell.

Then the person turns and she is glad she has her phone

out. For just a moment his face becomes clear. Josiah. As she suspected. She would need to get her hands on the vial to prove it as well. But first she needed to do something about Lovell and replace his IV back. If Josiah is doing what she suspects, the sooner Lovell is off his IV meds the better. The sooner he'll have a chance of recovering.

A noise draws both Josiah and her attention. Someone else entered the room.

"What are you doing here? I thought I was on shift."

One of the other doctors. She can't see which one and she doesn't recognize his voice.

"I was just checking on Lovell," Josiah says. But the syringe is still in his hand. No doubt the doctor noticed. Josiah tries to play it off by disposing of the syringe in the sharps container. But it is no use.

"Did you log that?"

Realizing what he meant, a smirk comes on Chloe's face. All the medications are being logged on the associated patient whiteboards and charts. Every single dosage. Josiah wouldn't record something dangerous. And no doubt he wasn't going to record it now.

"I was about to," Josiah says. He approaches the white board. Chloe realizes the board is between the two doctors and the distance between Josiah and the doctor has closed considerably.

Chloe realizes what Josiah is about to do a second before it happens. Josiah takes a swing at the doctor, knocking the man to the ground.

Her hand closes on a metal bedpan behind her. She tucks her phone into her pocket, praying to the gods and goddesses that it would not break. Then she moves.

As fast as her werewolf legs will carry her, she shoots out of the cabinet and closes the gap between herself and a shocked Josiah. She swings the bedpan at him, hitting him upside the head. The blow is nowhere near enough to knock him out, but it does buy a moment for the other doctor to get to his feet. It's Dr. Maurice Caulder. A werewolf from a neighboring pack who came in to help them. An ally.

Maurice tackles Josiah. The vial falls from his hand and Chloe seizes upon the opportunity to scoop it up.

"Run! Get help!" Maurice says.

The blows Josiah lands on him only spurs Chloe on to do what he says. So she turns tail and runs out of the ward and down the stairs to the front door.

The shock on the guards' faces at seeing her come out fades to anger when they register her words. Panting for breath and still clutching the bedpan, she hurriedly tells them what is happening. That Josiah is attacking Maurice. That he injected something into Lovell.

She holds up the vial when she tells them that part. The

guards rush past her into the house. Another doctor takes the vial in a gloved hand and reads it. The doctor swears comprehensively, turns to the remaining wolves.

"Go get that traitor and bring him here alive."

The sounds of a scuffle radiate out from the front door. A bang shakes the building. She hears the sounds of wolves going out the back door and running into the woods. It dawns on Chloe that Josiah is trying to escape into the night. He has a head start too.

"Chloe, you need to sit down. You're going to have to stay in the quarantine ward for a few days to determine if you were exposed," Dr. Renee Brommel says.

Chloe shakes her head. "He injected the vial's contents into Lovell's IV. It needs to be changed asap."

Renee considers her for a moment then turns to the nearest nurse. "Change all the IV lines, fluid and everything. Start new catheters. And give all the patients a fresh dose of antivirals," she barks out the orders with dire certainty.

Three nurses snap into action. Jarrod, the one nearest to them, snatches up a box with vials, presumably antivirals, and heads into the house with the other two trailing behind.

"Now sit," Renee says.

Exhausted, she can no longer argue. She takes a seat close to the doctor and does not remove her mask. She knows she's put herself at risk, but there's nothing she can do about it now except wait.

"I'm going to give you an injection of the latest antiviral serum we were sent from the CDC. Just to be safe. Then we're going to find you a bed downstairs and you're going to rest."

Chloe just nods. She doesn't protest even when the needle pierces her skin and she feels the fluid inject into her muscle.

"We can't trust anyone," is all she says.

Her phone lights up. It's a text from the group in Denver. *"Josiah Fredegund is a mole."*

Too late. He's already gone.

31

EVERY LAST ONE

"Too many got away," Kit says. "They had to have a lot of help to make all this data happen."

Kai peers over his shoulder as she reads the list of informant initials. "It's disgusting how many have turned against their own kind." She is still angry about Josiah Fredegund getting away. When Chloe told her that an hour ago and that the pack had put out a kill or capture order, she felt angry enough to want him to be killed. He killed Asa and that shouldn't go unpunished. But her logical side knows they could learn more from questioning him. She just wishes there was another way.

"They're everywhere too," Kit says. He lets out a tight sigh prompting Kai to squeeze his shoulder. Never would she have thought she'd be comforting a werewolf with techie tendencies.

A thought occurs to her. "Can you see if you can find any of their other facilities? I assume they have some."

Kit looks up at her with fear in his eyes. "I'll check now. It might take me a while to find them though. And I'll probably have to keep looking when we get back to Atlanta."

The werewolf proceeds to type away at the keyboard, his attention going back to the laptop. Around them in the kitchen the cleanup process is nearly done. No one will ever know they were even at the house if they do their jobs correctly. She knows upstairs the process is ongoing as well.

Kai straightens up and stretches her neck. The majority of people had left the house by now. The various teleporters had done a good job of getting them out of Denver proper. Some were already heading to Atlanta to get vaccinated at the CDC. She knew Greg Nixon had been working overnight along with the vampires to get that finished.

Kai wanders into the living room where Nicolette still rests on the couch. She would be in the last group to leave. Ezra felt it would be best to give her some time to rest before moving her. She took a lot of hits in the building and lost some blood. She looks a lot less pallid than she did before, but as Kai knows healing takes time.

Oriphine pops into view, having taken a group out of the house. The clock on the wall reads four in the morning. They don't have much time left.

"We should get the rest of them people out," Oriphine says. "How many are left?"

"Six I think, including Nicolette," she says gesturing to the vampire-witch on the couch.

As if the sound of her name revives her, Nicolette blinks awake and says, "I'm alright. We can go now."

Kai sits on the coffee table and examines Nicolette's shoulder. The vampire blood's healing properties have done a startlingly good job of closing the wound. She checks her leg as well, where the second bullet nearly severed her femoral artery. She would have died had Ezra not come to the house.

Satisfied the wounds are healed, Kai helps Nicolette sit up.

"Are you sure you're alright?"

"I'm ravenous, but otherwise alright," she answers. "I could go for a steak right about now."

"We'll get you one in Atlanta," Kai says, amused that the witch side is the hungry part.

Sirens in the distance draw their attention. The sound approaches and Kit comes into the living room with his laptop tucked under his arm.

"I saw lights in the neighbor's house. I think they might have called the cops."

"We should get out of here."

The last few werewolves and witches come down the stairs and join the group in the living room. "Did you get everything?" Oriphine asks them.

"We did," one of the witches answers.

"I'll set a go-back spell to go off when we leave. It'll reset any belongings to a week ago." Kai forms the spell in her head and in her heart. The idea came to her in the kitchen when she realized they had nearly used up all the paper towels. The spell would likely pull a new roll from a store somewhere, but that was better than finding the house disturbed.

She places her hand palm-down on the coffee table and lets the spell sit there with a sixty second timer. "We should go now."

The group, now accustomed to teleporting, links up to Oriphine, the last teleporting person in the house.

In one breath they are all gone and back in the CDC. Kai takes a few breaths, knowing the spell is about to draw on her energy. The kind of work she suggested takes its toll. The minute passes. She feels a distant tug and reaches for the nearest chair to sit down. She closes her eyes.

"Are you alright Kai?"

The voice belongs to Greg.

"She cast a pretty advanced spell when we left," someone, probably Oriphine, explains. "She needs some orange juice or something for her blood sugar."

"We have some," Greg says. Kai hears him rushing off.

A few minutes later someone puts a cup of something in her hand. She opens her eyes and ignores her spinning head long enough to drink the orange juice. Like with diabetes, magic can cause a rapid drop in blood sugar that causes witches to pass out. She hands the empty cup back to Greg and closes her eyes. The spell was definitely advanced, but not beyond her abilities. Just outside of her normal specialty.

There is a bustle of activity around her as she sits with her eyes closed for the next five minutes or so. When she opens them again, the majority of the witches and wolves are relaxing in the waiting area.

"Better?" This time the person asking is Nyxie. She had taken a seat across from Kai and was apparently waiting for her to come out of her sugar drop.

"A lot." Kai looks around in confusion. "Where is everyone?"

"The lab. Greg is going to start inoculating everyone at six. So they're getting ready. Everyone has been called in."

"What about those who got away?"

Nyxie's smile is far too evil for Kai's comfort level.

"We'll get them. Every last one."

A chill runs up Kai's spine.

"We better," she says darkly. *Or they'll just start again*, she adds silently.

Nyxie nods as if she heard Kai's thoughts.

"We will."

Kai sits back in her chair watching the creatures around her and wondering how long any of them really has.

32

"I HOPE YOU'RE WRONG"

Adin's phone goes off and wakes him up around four in the morning. He rolls over to see Lairlux waking slowly as well. She no longer hides her demon form around him, so he meets her brown eyes and gently caresses her reddish cheek. Then he checks his phone.

"Vaccines at 6AM."

The text is from Greg Nixon to the whole group. Several replies had chimed in that they are coming. Getting the group vaccinated meant they could go to places like the Swifttooth pack and start vaccinating those who had not yet been exposed to the virus. There are too many pockets of outbreaks that have already happened to wait for the vaccine to go through testing. Too many people dying to let this go.

"We have to go in to get vaccinated in two hours."

Lairlux pulls him back closer to her and says, "So that means we have two hours to snuggle before we have to go in."

"For a half demon you are particularly cuddly," he says amused.

She kisses his shoulder and whispers, "For a big tough werewolf, so are you."

Adin rolls over and kisses her deeply, passionately. His phone goes off again. He groans emphatically but checks it.

"That's Oriphine offering to pick us up in thirty minutes."

Lairlux grumbles something about "punctual spirits" being annoying. She just snuggles closer to Adin and refuses to let go. He doesn't resist.

About thirty minutes later they pull themselves out of bed, Adin heading to the shower. For once Lairlux joins him. They take their time getting ready to go and by the time Adin texts Oriphine to come get them it is after five o'clock.

The spirit pops into their living room with a bemused expression on her face. She doesn't make any remark on their tardiness despite Adin suspecting what she's holding back.

"Ready?" is all she asks.

A minute later they are walking through the staff break

room at the CDC and marveling at the ridiculous number of people who have taken up residence. There must be thirty creatures waiting at this wee hour of the morning for Greg Nixon to administer vaccines to them.

Hand in hand, Adin and Lairlux find Kai and the rest waiting down the hall.

"Have you heard the news?"

"Which part?"

"About the mole," Kai says impatiently.

Adin pulls out his phone. Buried in the messages is a single line of text that shocks him to his core. Lairlux swears as she reads it as well.

"We're almost certain he killed Asa," Kai continues. "Chloe was already on to him when we messaged her. She exposed herself to the virus to prove her theory. She is currently in quarantine."

Adin looks through the windows into the breakroom and shakes his head. "If someone like Josiah Fredegund could be a mole, I shudder to think who else could be one."

"We've alerted all the clusters," Kai adds, "but I fear it will bring out paranoia and panic."

"Oh for certain," Lairlux says. "I think part of this is getting creatures to turn against each other."

"We don't need help to do that," Adin mutters. "We've been doing better in the recent weeks, but once this passes,

I'm afraid we'll all fall into our old ways."

"I hope you're wrong."

"I hope I am too," Adin answers.

For a moment no one says anything. Adin watches the comings and goings of the group with a vague feeling of suspicion now. How many of them do they really know? And will they ever be able to trust each other again?

"It's time."

Greg calls out to them from the doorway down the hall. Kai leaves them to go back into the break room and begin rounding up contenders for the vaccine. Adin can't do more than lean against the wall with Lairlux's hand in his.

"We'll find them," she whispers.

He looks into her eyes, eyes that flash red for just a moment.

He kisses her and nods his head.

"We'll find them," he agrees.

33

ONE DROP

Greg inserts a needle in the vial and draws out a milliliter of the fluid. He extracts the needle and taps the syringe once, twice, and then puts a cap over the needle. He repeats the process six more times as he waits for the crew to be ready for vaccinations. They don't have enough time to go through testing procedures, but he feels confident that the vaccine can do its job. This would never pass for human trials, but humans don't need this nearly as much as the creatures do.

Ezra steps into the lab then and doesn't say anything, just begins drawing up syringes as well. They have a crowd to vaccinate and only so much time to do it in. It is just a good thing that the vampire brought so much knowledge to the table. Ezra had helped them find a way to mass produce this new vaccine in such a small lab. They had sixteen vials before them, enough to hit everyone in the waiting room once. Behind him on the lab bench, a centrifuge mixed the next batch of vials. Next to the centrifuge, another sixteen vials of concentrated vaccine stood at the ready to be taken to the hot spots around the globe.

"We should get other labs in on this, shouldn't we?" Greg says.

"I'm not sure," the vampire Prince says. "If we can't trust our own people, then who can we trust with this?"

Greg finishes off the vial he is using and sets the empty container down, capping the needle and setting it down as well. Ezra comes to a pause and looks at him. "A month ago if you told me I would be standing in my lab with a vampire Prince, drawing up a vaccine to protect creatures against a genetically modified virus, I would have called you delusional," he says. "But I wouldn't go back now." He reaches over and just for an instance squeezes Ezra's hand. He isn't that tactile, but he felt the need to touch the vampire's cool skin right then.

The moment passes and Greg picks up one of the prepared syringes. "You first," he says. "I'm not taking chances that it'll break through your vampire immune system."

Ezra gives him a wry smile. "You do care," he teases. But the vampire rolls up his sleeve and presents his arm to Greg.

The lab door opens and Kai comes in. "Leave some for the rest of us," she says with a glint in her eye. "They're ready. Do you want to do this here or out there?"

"Out there," Greg says. "Out is always better than in."

Ezra snorts. Greg hands him a Hello Kitty bandaid which Ezra, despite not needing it, puts on over the vaccine wound. The injection site has already healed but he proudly displays his bandaid for Kai.

"It suits you," she says with a laugh. Greg realizes it's the first time he heard Kai laugh since the news of Asa's death.

Kai is piling the prepared syringes into plastic trays to take out to the break room. When they are filled and every syringe is packed, she hands one of the trays to Greg and one to Ezra. "Make yourselves useful, boys." She takes the third tray and heads out of the lab.

"I am useful."

"Witches, I swear," Ezra says with a laugh and a roll of the eyes.

"Will you be able to contain yourself?" Greg asks, waggling his eyebrows at Ezra and indicating the syringes.

"While yes, I can smell even one drop of blood, I can control myself," he answers. "One drop of vaccine is far more important than one drop of blood right now."

"Then let's get to it."

Together they walk down the hall to the break room. They set up three tables for creatures to get their vaccines. They even have Oriphine at the ready in case there is a reaction. But the injections go smoothly. And Greg looks around, the lone human in a room full of creatures.

Ezra catches his eye and raises an empty syringe to him.

"Here's to the end," the vampire jokes about his last vaccine to administer.

Greg smiles. He administers the last vaccine in his batch. Looking around at all the creatures with Hello Kitty bandaids, he feels what Ezra's words really mean. This is the moment. This is the beginning of the end of the plague.

ABOUT THE AUTHOR

Olivia "Lollie" Jones Black has been writing in some form or other since she was eleven. Her writing provides an emotional and creative outlet during this chaotic time. With work spanning a broad range of themes and worlds, she brings the reader to places both familiar and far away.

A background in science provides inspiration for her work. Her writing blends both science fiction and fantasy, epic and mundane. Her other books include *Altair* and *Linguist*.

A cat who thinks she owns the computer occasionally helps with the writing. She lives on the east coast.

Made in the USA
Middletown, DE
18 June 2023